Jam

MW00723922

A fictional journey of a young man with poor traits, to an old man, the artist without portraits.

By

Leon O'Chruadhlaoich

(Unabridged)

Pisces Press Publishing Company
Dallas, Texas, USA

Library of Congress Cataloging-in-Publication Data
O'Chruadhlaoich, Leon, 1942-
    James Joyce : A fictional journey of a young man with poor traits, to
    an old man, the artist without portraits. / Leon O'Chruadhlaoich.

Library of Congress Control Number: 2004102012
ISBN-10: 1-888426-14-4
ISBN-13: 978-1-888426-14-4

Attention: Quantity discounts are available on bulk purchases of this book.
For information contact:
Marketing Department, Pisces Press Publishing Company
Phone: 214-739-8675
Fax: 214-368-2238
E-mail: leomcrowley@yahoo.com

Second Edition
10 9 8 7 6 5 4 3 2 1
Published by Pisces Press Publishing Company

Pisces Press Publishing Company
P.O. Box 670492,
Dallas,
Texas 75367-0492.

Acknowledgements

This work is a written testimony to the unconditional support of Carol Chappelear B.A., David Lewis M.D., and Rosemary O'Neill R.N., whose collective and immense literary wisdom, poetical knowledge, philological insights, worldly etymology and words of appreciation and encouragement made it all possible.

To my beloved father, Mathew, in whom I am well pleased, four *chillun* he rears, fortune for seers, forty all-wonderful literary years, poetical tears, un-forgettable peers, forgettable fears, de railleur gears, never-heard jeers, ever-ready ears, never-seen leers, happy-time beers, but as transition-time nears, the long lifeline veers, the short lifetime disappears, witness the unrequited tears over his never-ending, undying, ever-faithful marriage of over 60 years to my late, loving, living, laughing, poetry-talking, Glendyne Wood walking, darling, dearly-departed, delightful, delectable, dearest mother, Matilda Crowley (nee Connors).

"Last night the moon had a golden ring, tonight no moon we see......"

-The Wreck of the Hesperus

Back Words

Whether back words, forwards, Fore ! Woods, Tiger would, backwards, four words, well words, sick wards, backwoods, firewood, dire words, black woods, whitewash, gray words, bare-back, threadbare sacks, brown bears, wood-bare shacks, sat a throne, stare at the night stand, stand alone at the stair, strain at the *barre*, sink in the quicksand, swim in the sink, what's there to think, yet now rises again the next great writer and wrong-doer, artist and do-righter, inadvertently sent from such a loverly land to banishment, head hung down in the tightening rope of famishment, yet not a dull Erin-man from the *Dail Eireann* clan ever knew what famished meant, always immune from the well-fed Talisman, hallways opportune in the Al Queda-led Taliman, and even after leaving *The Field*, Bull McCabe painfully pointed out to us all that nary a single, well-fed, mother-led, stutter-said, butter-bread, litter-read, never-wed, Jesus dead, uncle Ned, sashes red, Parish priest ever perished in *The Famine*. Joyless poison in the altar wine, and nothing to re-Joyce about here.

Despite it all, Ireland's laughter is the music of the spheres reduced to the point of audibility, it's *Book of Kells* the beauty of the Gods seduced to the point of visibility, the cries of it's martyrs deduced to the point of verbal versatility, the mental telepathy of it's writers re-juiced to the point of legibility, it's pen-ultimate fate the voice of the Joycean prophet crying out on top of the hobbit-bare *Burren*, sighing aloud across the gray-granite *boreen*, a barren-bare bear roaming Prince Erin's green land, a warren-lair hare honing Princess Eireann's lean hand, roaming in the gloaming through untidy bowers of rampant flowers, fuming and foaming around crumbling stone towers, their fingernail wall-scraped writings wet-draped in cowers, homegrown under Dublin's dreary gray showers, the *Scholastic Irishman* bone-honed in Rathgar's city-rat dowers, the rogue-docent descendancy and brogue-nascent ascendancy with despoiling God's intimate tendency to pull hares out of hats, hairs out of heads, perch linguistic leprechauns with peat-pounding *bodhrans* hazing and amazing o'er grazing fairy-garden lawns, the Mad Hatter and Alice 'midst the mad chatter and chalice, so much sensuous sensitivity and deciduous civility in Ireland's great proclivity, and yet immature and sinful, a drunk with a skin-full, a beggar with a tin full, the parsing Poet of Dublinic divinity was pasted and plastered, Belvedere'd and mastered, and stood tall in the squall of that reclusive vicinity. His great contribution, an act of retribution, was the "Day of Rabblement" toilet the rabble of cryptic critics *know* what babble meant. Nothing to re-Joyce about here, either.

Yet with the *Anam Cara* of such persuasiveness, the ancient and mystical Celtic Gods of such pervasiveness, the *croags* of ancient Hibernia of such elated enlightenment, Ireland's lore a place of persistent wonderment where God's gifts are sown with infinite penance meant, the oral Celtic farmer scattering seeds across his field flatulent, the Oracle Delphic charmer with his yield supplement; all a cross to bear, a crucifix to bare, *un croix a guerre*, all ever all-mindful of the winds that pass inevitably over the reasoned seasons of our life and the seasoned reasons of our souls. *James Joyce must have known it all at one time or another.* The world is made up of God's infinitesimal handiwork, a seamless garment of indelible hue, occasionally laced with wickedness and treachery, but nevertheless full of magic, enchantment, minor miracles and inexplicable delights, perhaps calling us all back to that enchanted isle with which both God and Joyce were so disenchanted. At the end of it all, both pall-bearers of appall. Despite the "please" of modern-day bribes, the pleas of the auld ancient tribes, the bribes of the latter-day scribes, the plans of the clans, the wrecks of the sects, the collects of the Celts, the gales of the Gaels, and the incest of Ireland's ancestors, Joyce never went back. It was a King's promise, and one that He never broke.

Deadication

May the eclectic gathering of the articulate minority, the dyslectic gathering of the attention deficit disordered, the functioning and sub-clinical schizophrenics, the intellectual misfits, wayward writers, polemic poets, water-color painters, un-published publicans, indiscriminate pelicans, literate housewives with their pots and pans, illiterate bee-keepers with their honey pans, honeys' with their Dapper Dan's, the insanely mundane, the moribund insane, the marital inane, the voices of the prophets crying in the wilderness, the choices of the profits trading with the guilder-less, tiki-torched in the night-fires with the manatees, pity-scorched in the bonfire of the insanities, any ignored Noble with a novella, any deplored Nobel in a bordello, even an ignoble Noble with a non-Nobel novel, whoever left a life to grovel with the righteous in the un-published hovel, and who in naval uniform contemplates the navel of Evel Knievel ? We are all auctioned off cheaply to a thankless crowd at one time or another before being saluted by the Confederate Army of dunces, the confectionate armchair of lunches, the inconvenient barmy of bunches, the inconsiderate wrong air of hunches, forever, for always, grafiti in the hallways, leaving a write-full trace in the wrong-full place in the suffocating midst of our boring, snoring, goring and whoring critics.

Table of Contents

James Joyce

Go Mbeanni Dea duit agus Failte Romhat.

The Gods up in the Heavens, they made all the Irish mad; and for all their wars they're happy, and for all their songs they're sad. But such Foley copyrighted neuro-linguistics and solely poppy-sighted linguistic phrasiology cannot be sanctimoniously holy to the Great Gods themselves (*They* would deliver Him if He delighted in Hymn), *They* have to look around for a suitable mortal to introduce less lexical polyconics, more semantic polygonics, somewhat phototonic representations, more or less clerical planktonics, less or more syntaxial polytonics, intermittent agrammatical isogonics, persistently syntactic isotonics, employing the structural enjoyment of the lower rabble illegally inhabiting the ex-Tower of Babel without ever destroying the distractional employment of the upper rabble legally exhibiting the sex-power of Scrabble. Thus, Nature's Man-plan for Mr Joyce, a literary choice, a Rolls Royce of words, an effigy of eloquivalence, a tumescence of eloquence, a rural sural, an urban with a turban, a talisman with a Tallit shawl, a Manshevik amongst the

Bolsheviks, an inquisitorious anti-hero, an meritorious Auntie hero, acitizen-denizen, a foundation of the Nation, a publican Republican, a democratic diplomat, a penmanship phenomenon, a Zenwomanboat prolegomenon, the lexicon from Lexington, no dimwit, nitwit, halfwit or dim Mick from Limerick; a documented Kipling stripling, and not even Captain Ahab's tear at Patricio's or Yap Stam's gear at Lazio nor all the water in the Pacific swell contained such wealth, nor all the fire in horrific Hell maintained such stealth from Bethel Herman Melville's Moby Dick to Ethel Merman's Hellville Mick Doby as was in *His* pen, where the ink of the *Scholastic Irishman* far outlived the blood of the Catholic martyrs, rewriting pages of Sages, absentmindedly scribbling in Sears about Seers, and became very much requited and simply delighted to enlighten His audiences, voluminously writing for those stumbling of speech and forever profusely talking for those limping of tongue, and yet columninously spiting those tumbling into leech and five-never robustly walking into primping of dung (only San Andreas has more faults). He was a literary Deity in the Highest, a poetic nicety on the quiet, a prosaic sobriety on a diet, articulating for the notoriety of Notary slick to try it but without a sophisticate society quick to buy it; a Mark Cuban Czar with an pantry pastry, a dark Cuban cigar with an astray ashtray; He chased the Indian out of the cupboard, came out of the closet to put the State in a state, left Bath for a shower, went into Hollingshed, met Thomas Tallis in Tallin, bet Robert Oppenheimer in Berlin, let Odysseus be called *Ulysses* in Latin, traded in His Irish tweed for satin, waded into C. K. Stead's *The New Poetic* and became instead the *askew phonetic*, was jaded with C. S. Lewis's "dark embryo" of unconscious energy and faded into the "stark dynasty" of sub-conscious synergy, in *Finders Keepers* (page 41) raided "everything is beginning, the most satisfying recovery is greeting, the *borreen* of negative bereavement leads to the *diva positiva*." And with that His right temporal lobe left Him with persistent hypergraphia, and He succumbed to bread crumbs, surrendered to chicken tenders and fought off Alice Flaherty's midnight disease on a daily basis. He wore a chlamys made of *chamois*, whore a chlamydia Sade de Marquis, complimented Hermione in her ermine, dedicated an obelisk in Minsk, became the un-disciplined Disciple, feared by the irrelevant Reverends as the "wrath of Rathgar," revered by the relevant deviants where the river ends as "the spar of deodar," an Edwardian historian, a non-hibernate Hibernian, a cyber-mate Iberian, a brotherly Cistercian, a parsimonious Persian, a very clear Confucian, a crucified Rosicrucian, an intoning Solomonic,

a beatnik Slavic, a synoptic Coptic, a macrocosmic Cosmic,
a flowing Danubian, a flame-throwing Nubian, an andante
Dante, a biblical Vedantic, an agnostic Christian Barnard,
wrote twiddling Irish prose about piddling English pro's,
watched Christopher robbin' Alice in her Mad Hatter
place at the Palace, ate a plaice with His salad, was never
a sad lad, had time on his hands, watched Stephen age in
Stephenage, disliked bosuns who handled bosoms, liked "go
sons" who felt 'em in Feltham, loved brass bands, adored
Ceili bands, waved intuition to Bart, paved percipience in
a cart, gave discernment to art, bathed with water a quart,
laid clairvoyance on an incredible sham tart, ate divination
off an edible jam tart, Dave'd precognition with cartoon-
character Garth, prayed divination with all His heart, made
sagacity on city-bus DART, saved oodles of noodles at the
Super-Sam Mart, caved Hay Wain with a boatswain upstart,
prayed in the Nave for His soul to depart, raved portent
in a tent set apart, shaved augury off a wart, He carted His
books, darted His board, kind-hearted His nice nieces (He
loved them to pieces), K-Marted His shoes, tarted His oven
and meant nothing aromatic as He inadvertently farted
as He silently departed the romantic part of His Paris
apartment. His an "all alone" allotheism, a multitude of one,
a part of the Catholic orthodoxy, apart from the Protestant

cacodoxy, depart the Jewish heterodoxy, art of the literature paradoxy, a non-Irishman by proxy, rowed an Irish *curragh* without coxy, rode a stylish Harley most foxy, wrote a Sura most doxy, became a discount Viscount, a Harlem Globetrotter, an Elizabeth Hurley bogtrotter, a Humphrey *bogey-man* bog-trotting with a hurley, always the Lamb of Judah from the neat Dublin house-loft who ever-met Sultans and Mullahs but never met the "Lion of Judah," the Bolton Nat Lofthouse.

Qui gravis es nimium, potes hinc iam, lector, abire quo libet.

Always the Buddha of Barbuda, an arable parable, a comedic curmudgeon, a Gideon pigeon, a dethroning Brythonic, a bemoaning Housatonic, a postponing Adonic, a disowning Aaronic, a groaning Amphictyonic, a cataphonic Chalcedonic, an enthroning Pyrrhonic, a stoning Metonic, a nondescript *nom-de-plume,* a bibliopolist of the acropolis, a metropolite of the cosmopolis, a monoploist of the Heliopolis, a pharmacopolist of the megalopolis, a cosmopolite of the metropolis, a mutineer with scrutineer, a bibliomaniacal academical, a prodigal ventriloquial, a Sarawak with a plaque, a proverbial professor, a mother confessor, an ambidexterous dexiotrope, a lazy laeotrope, dexter and sinister, dextrorse and

5

sinistrorse, profound and terrific, ascetic and prolific, a non-
Serb acerbic, an eclectic dyslectic, an Etonian phenologist,
a Harrowing phrenologist, a bezonian most catatonical, a
Favonian penologist, a fer-de-lance with insouciance, *now an*
old man, the artist without portraits, once a young man with
poor traits, a press man not a "yes" man, a herbalist verbalist,
a pluralist ruralist, *always* a journalist eternalist, had voracious
audacity, consuming capacity, didactic *dicacity,* bellicose
feracity, dissentious bellacity, a chemisette bibacity, a *facile*
edacity, meaningless fugacity, incredible incapacity, infrequent
loquacity, tremendous mendacity, portentous minacity, lively
mordacity, impregnable opacity, delightful perspicacity,
outrageous pertinacity, edentulous pervicacity, contradictory
procacity, Quaker pugnacity, rambunctious rapacity, uplifting
sagacity, Japanese saponacity, premeditated sequacity,
reversible tenacity, voracious veracity, post-mortem vivacity,
a veracious voracity before chasing curvaceous chastity, was
sure and azure, verse and asperse, always delighted to visit the
lily-white Lillie White in her vanilla villa, not yet a win-gent but
Sir Taintly A strin-gent, an un-heard of voice, an un-bearded
choice, played the Swiss alpenhorn with Chris Langenhorne,
played insightfully in Blighty forlorn, made love with an
English mistress on the French horn, strayed delightfully
brightly with much single distress when to a Catholic wench

born, frayed wheat with the *Children of the Corn*, laid neat
rows of barleycorn, made the weasels go "pop" in the popcorn,
ate salt with peppercorn, fed the hee-haw donkeys hawthorn,
led Charlie Haughey around the Matterhorn, made short work
of the longicorn, when buckthorn at the rodeo stayed skyborne,
in the ocean sailed cloud-borne, lawfully mistook a potion
when forlorn, unlawfully Miss Took a *Goshun* in video porn,
a motion in soft porn, a commotion in hard porn, and played
and remained outwardly plaid, cowardly staid, unforgivably
forbade, saw through the charade, and made Florida's County
Dade outlaw the masquerade of the kiddie-porn trade. *Quis
custodiet ipsos custodes ?*

A most saintly Joyce, Deus ex machina.

He was an accolade from Adelaide, an Aberdonian zoologist,
an enzymologist most acronycal, an Amazonian universologist,
a craniologist most antochronical, an Ammonian typologist,
a biologist most antichronical, an Aonian therologist,
a zymologist most iconical, an Ausonian theologist, a
scientologist most harmonical, an aseptic skeptic, He laughed
uproariously at Kenneth Horne, sailed another *curragh*
around the rape of Cape Horn, prayed a *Sura* around the
nape of the firstborn, the prairie-hands made up fairy tales for
greenhorns but with Mary made up hairy tails forlorn, added

7

white sauce to the fast-sloe of the blackthorn, was sympathetic to the unborn, peripatetic to the trueborn, reacted violently to the stillborn, always moonlighted for the day-born, was swoon-sighted for the night-born, broom-plighted for the heaven-born, looked down on the highborn, looked up to the low-born, went out with the inborn, went golfing with a hunting horn, dined in on trout very sea-born, wined out of a priming horn, roasted beef in a drinking horn, would forewarn with a fog-horn, scorn with pew disadorn, re-adorn with new "this a dorm," at old wasp-frames would bescorn, at cold Wasps games would be warm, out of rugby-bold WASPS would pull thorns, and with a trace of self-scorn, would recite will-I-am-shake-his-spear, who like the unicorn of *yestermorn* "would drink old wine and love forlorn, then rue the headache of the morn." He worked undercover whilst Nora worked undercovers, they were both left un-covered by Peter Blake's cover which was literally adorned with the adored *literati* including Alas ! A stair Crowley, Edgar Allen Poet, Aldous the Hukster, Karl Marks the Spot, Dhomas Tylan, Great Britain Shaw, wild Oscar Wilde, Lewis and Clark Carroll, and Tea Lawrence, to have and to hold, and now this latter literary genius (I wish *He* could have seen us) we now adorn with many tokens, the survivor of many adventures and the witness of many miracles, always read but never met the Buddha on the road, was once involved in a paternity suit (very neat) and twice made a visit to the maternity suite (very sweet) with the news in the pews, amidst crews of shrews, a cruise full of brews, fighting the militia *Druse*, dues paid by Jews, to a muse with a ruse, a Sue who'd been sued, you'd be viewed at the zoo, wooed by the lewd, with the news shouted aloud to the quarrelsome queues dressed in torrid-some hues in the rabble-strewn *rues*.

A *drop of the crathure.*

He was a languishing Irish Anglophobe, an English Language treasure-trove, a victorious Ambassador, an ambassadorial Victorian, was very skittish around the British, very tinglish around the English, sipped leek soup with the Welsh, would wax-on with the Anglo-Saxons, was very yachtish around the Scottish, not a stylish kilt and sporran but Irish-built and foreign, always drinking massive masses of molasses with Parnell et al at the Mount Parnassus parnassus, avoided risky whiskey but would enjoy Scott's whiskey, Scotch whisky or even a Scot's whiskey with the Scots' lower classes or bell-weather clinking passive glasses of Scottish Scotch with the Scots' upper lassies, became livid with strapping Glen in the stripling glen when observed toppling after tippling *Glenlivet;* rigid-sized Glen in the widget-prized glen would fidget with his hard wood in the bark-strewn, greenwood glade

before nibbling and nippling on Bridget in the dark-brown,
wildwood shade; and while waiting for a waiter to wait on
Him became very kin-ish in wee Yeats' bee-loud glade, all-
the-while whittling and whistling, whispering and whimpering,
winnowing and wintering, witnessing and wearying, wakening
and wandering, weathering and weakening, whinnying and
wondering, wantoning and wassailing, watering and wavering,
westering and worrying on and on until the *Glenfiddich* was
blessed in the glen by Rabbi Glenn Fiddich, was drunk by
the Yiddish, and was definitively finished by the famished
Finnish. Now James Cagney-sized Glen would move Angie
with *Glenmovangie,* she would disrobe after *Glenrothes,* his
dear hard wood in the deer guard wood weird-wedded in the
torrid-red daylight, bedded on the forest-bred nightshade,
with the platypus duck-billing, the spider monkeys milling,
the jolly birds trilling, the dolly-birds making a killing with a
"shot" for a shilling, the pulp-writers quilling, the thrushes
in bushes or just window-silling, the farmers stopped tilling,
and with "deep throat" Angie most willing, deep-drilling
Glen was moaning and foaming in a manner most thrilling.
He now herded all the lowland ponies who would stink and
Dal-whinny, and nerded all his highland cronies who wood
drink brand *Dalwhinnie;* drank *Balvenie* at Belvedere, drunk
Tyrconnell with sober Tyrone O'Connell, made Winnie the

Pooh booped and Betty Boop pooped, for Glen was a cinch to get the grinch in a pinch for more *Glenkinchie,* an Adventist dentist got doctor Grogan to grog on more on the foggy moor in the foggy dew and a Lentist fencist got proctor Craig not to drag much more through the doggy door despite the more cracks, craigs, carraigs, creags, crages, cragges, crags and crevices of the interminable *craic* on the craggy *Cragganmore.* More *Tullamore Dew* was due at Tullamore, less *Abelour* was drunk on Ilkley Moor, James's son was sent for more *Jameson's*, whiskey addicts would kill begging for more *Kilbeggan*, and *Famous Grouse* twice made an infamous louse out of Robert Burns who licked a sample of whisky *Red Breast* off Nelly Kilpatrick's ample white breast as he penned her "*O Once I Lov'd*" and hen pinned her to the crest of Mayo's Croagh Patrick. Sober brewers on dray horses drank *Powers Gold Label* while drunk queuers on day courses stank Johnny Power's old table, the Mills Brothers were ambushed in bushes for their *Bushmills*, Hugh Grant's grant at Oxford was celebrated with *Grants*, there are more old rare whiskies in Middleton than *Middleton Old Rare*, drunken rogues after Schnapps take naps at *Knappogue Castle*, John Balfour sipped *Abelour* with the poor on his rabble-tour, whiskey-tasters dilly and dally-more with their silly and *Dalmore*, you can't knock and do nothing after a bottle of *Knockando*, and after barrels

11

and pints of *Balvenie Cardhu* the Gardai will card you. They sent to Coventry for Gary Pallister to get them more *Talisker,* to France for an field athlete who would throw *le javelin* and then throw them more *Lagavulin,* sent Alan to McAllen, Texas for more *Macallan;* chugged *Chivas Regal* with the Royals, lugged *Crown Royal* with the Regals, hugged the Regal Chivas of Mexico, bugged the Royal Crowns of Europe, drank *Courvoisier* with Lavoisier, sipped *Cointreau* with Count Reaux, tabled *Red Label* with swell black merchants, labeled *Black Label* with well bred Red Indians, drank *Johnnie Walker* with Perrier water with Muddy Waters in Louisiana, ranked bonnie talkers with Harrod's porters in Clearwater, Florida, drank *Glen Ord* in Fort Ord 'til drunk like a skunk, but *Our Man* in Havana had a go at the Alamo, He captured Santa Ana's bandana, ate his Mexican bananas, retired to Savannah and offered a drachm of *Drambuie* to Jim Bowie with "have a dram, Bowie." Now't can be denied from mid-England's Stratford-on-Avon to newts on south Scotland's Strathclyde, you can relay a fifth of *Bourbon* for display on the Firth of Clyde, or blurb on the relay o'er the Firth of Forth, observe the Scottish drink Scotch, the Scots' out-drink the Sassenachs, out-dink the Sassamids, out-wink the Sarmatians, out-think the J.P. Sartreans, out-ink the satirists, out-blink the Sardinians, out-link the satellites, out-mink the sartorials, out-kink the aboriginals, out-slink the Saracens, out-sink their own plumbers, out-sync the Satyrs, *In Sync* the rappers, out-fink the Saturnians, out-jink the Sasquatch, out-pink the Saurischians, out-zinc the Satsumas, out-rink the Dallas Stars, or just ask what frisky-frilled, biscuit-filled, mischief-killed, lispy-willed, trill-thrilled, whisky-spilled, whisker-tilled, window-silled, smutty-putty clerk would overdose on *Cutty Sark* in an over-fit, grass-knit under-lit park ? Easier to swallow *Oban* in Oman than in the Preston Hollow dark, drank Murphy's Stout with stout Murphy and pressed on hollow bark, and always wondered who duck-billed "hillbilly" Billy Hill and the Old Bailey's Billy Bailey for their bar bills, their public bar *Bailey's* bills, their legal Old Bailey bar quills, their pharmacy bar daily pills, and then lifted their barbells, flirted with bar belles, ran up their bar bills, rang on their bar bells, Bill's bar bills were unpaid and so it's no bloody wonder they rang the bell slow in Belfast. Three for a child, six for a woman and nine for a man. *Fin de siecle.*

Exposure to Scientific Religiosity and Worldly Medicine.

Now our Joycean Hero, always an accessorial valedictorian without xenoglossophobia, an amatorial stentorian without stygiophobia, a sartorial Senatorian without selachophobia, an authorial salutatorian without didaskaleinophobia, a conspiratorial purgatorian without anthropophobia,

13

a clamatorial praetorian without kakorrhiaphobia, an assertorial oratorian without pogonophobia, a memorial Nestorian without catagelophobia, a Manorial mid-Victorian without philematophobia, a pictorial marmorean without gephyrophobia, a sectorial hyperborean without spheksophobia, a scriptorial historian without enochlophobia, a heck of a Hectorian without opthalmophobia, a great Gregorian without ereuthophobia, a combatorial gladiatorian without arachnophobia, a compromissorial dictatorian without medomalacuphobia, an inquisitorial consistorian without tapinophobia, a legislatorial censorian without teratophobia, a phantasmagorial Bosporian without pteronophobia, a speculatorial amatorian without cainolophobia, a gray Dorian without ranidophobia, a Hungarian czigany without scorodophobia, an infralapsarian Calvinist without phasmophobia, both provocative and avocative without vacciniphobia, desperate and asperate without venereophobia, fantastic and atavistic without psychophobia, an atomic atonic without rhytidophobia, a Bohemian Athenian with a trace of schism but without Russophobia, a phenomena of synchronism without doraphobia, a prolegomena of achromatism without harpagophobia, a paean of anachronism without batrachophobia, a palliation of metachronism without coulrophobia, a paralipomena of chromatism

without trichopathophobia, an antilegomena of diplomatism
without atelophobia; a burgeoning bourgeon without
keraunothnetophobia, a totally assuming assymptote without
merinthophobia, a periphrasis persiflage without optophobia,
ever-ever aver, never a wordless cadaver, never average
but ever-aged, a proper protagonist without Sinophobia,
a Sovietologist *oxygonial* without aphenphosmphobia,
a doubtful deuteragonist without pnigerophobia,
a thereologist testimonial without chionophobia, a
Gorgonean paroemiologist without chromatophobia, a
sarcologist santimonial without aurophobia, a Grandisonian
parapsychologist without iatrophobia, a Sinologist patrimonal
without acarophobia, a Heliconian pantheologist without
cymobphobia, a micropaleontalogist monial without
barophobia, an Ionian orologist without kenophobia, a
sexologist most matrimonial but without gynephobia,
a Johnsonian opthalmologist without pathophobia, an
etymologist most demonial without pharmacophobia, a
laconian ontologist without odontophobia, a British Empirist
most colonial but without Francophobia, a Lapponian
numismatologist without molsmophobia, a Byron Nelsonist
most Colonial without Negrophobia, a Livonian musicologist
without ochlophobia, a technologist most ceremonial but
without thermophobia, a Macedonian monologist without

Germanophobia, an arch-type archeologist most Baronial
yet without crystallophobia, a Miltonian metapsychologist
without pediculophobia, a paleontologist inter-colonial
without parasitophobia, a Deucalion among the dandelions, a
diactinic diaspora without dysmorphophobia, a multitude of
one, the monogamous James (how real), the deuterogamical
Eugene (O'Neill), an apocryphal deuterocanonical without
dermatophobia, cute and astute but without cypridophobia,
avid and rabid but without agoraphobia, severe and
austere without stasibasiphobia, auspicious and suspicious
without aichmophobia, practical and axiomatical but
without mechanophobia, the abolitionist diabolist without
dextrophobia, a dyslectic therapeutical without ochlophobia, a
dialectic diageotropist without climacophobia, had arrogance
and assonance but without acousticophobia, a foliage diallage
without algophobia, a Myrmidonian lithologist without
maieusiophobia, an absolvable acknowledger without
alcoholophobia, a Neronian lexicologist without necrophobia,
a dissolvable astrologer without spectrophobia, a Newtonian
ideologist without necrophobia, an indissolvable sockdolager
without scotophobia, a Lady Oxonian gynecologist, a
male Cambridgian guy-knee-college-ist, an insolvable
osteologer without onomatophobia, a Patagonian horologist
without proctophobia, a resolvable botanologer without

bromidosiphobia, a Plutonian hagiologist rhabdophobia, an acarologist most ironical but without osphresiophobia, a Pyrrhonian glottologist without gymnophobia, an agrobiologist most Sorbonical without siderodromophobia, a Sardonian glossologist without hypengyophobia, an agrostologist most synchronical but without pecattiphobia, a Serbonian ethnologist without trichopathophobia, an anthropologist most tautophonical yet without triskaidekaphobia, a Simonian entomologist without Zenobia, an audiologist most tonical yet without ataxiophobia, a Slavonian deontologist without parasitophobia, an axiologist most thrasonical but without kleptophobia, a Thessalonian cryobiologist without thalassophobia, a bacteriologist most synchronical but without ataxiophobia, an agriologist most Babylonical but without entomophobia, a Usonian cosmologist without thanatophobia, a protozoologist most pharmaceutical with protagonistic nail cuticles yet without hamartophobia, played Association Football down Chelsea way with Mario Melchiot, the King of Arabia; flayed disassociation goofballs on Keller Kasey day with Caspar the Ghostly King of Tarsus, and prayed coronational, brayed dissertational, frayed terminational, grayed presentational, hayed irrigational, okayed informational, laid gravitational, made a maid incubational, nayed imitational, paid denominational, Denis

17

Quaid compensational, raid confrontational, Port Said salutational, waded bogs with Wade Boggs inspirational, was jaded with Jade vocational, and all in a heavenly way with Balmy Czar, the King of Ethiopia. He was forever the younger Alderman without Anglophobia, a baccalaureate in botany with indescribable flora, a George W. Bush with a Texas Laura, speaking of Texas how about a Dr Alexander Cora, even the *Quare Fella* had an aunt (now deceased) in Youghal, Ireland by the name of Crowley Dora, an Irish ex-girlfriend called Maura, please do mention the *Scholastic Irishman's* Barnacle Nora, how about a Japanese acquaintance who had a bit-part in Tora ! Tora !, or a Tahitian grass-skirt dancer from Bora Bora, in Romania and Israel they still dance the *hora*, but no pale-in-Rome Attick ever get a Handel on, or hold a candle to, the palindromic J.A.A.J., a true Poet Laureate with a Kirlian aura. *Also spracht Zaratustra.*

Introduction to the Planetary Horoscope.

He was a Babylonian teleologist, a geologist most geophonical, a Baconian sociologist, a diabologist most diaphonical, He went Karl Marx inane and spent German Marks insane on the *bealoga* with the family Spencer in Dublin's Marks and Spencer's, remarked Mark Twain on the jetty, "marked 'twain" in the Liffey, thought the "Generation X-ers" in O'Connell

Street always looked "spiffy," ate *ceapaire* at the Gresham but found the Toff's didn't give toffees, had *milseog* at Dewry's but found the Jews didn't give dowries, and after every *Priomh Cursa* drank a dewar of Irish Whisky. He would answer questions, question answers, then gave gestures to jesters but never answers to Chaucer, gave cups of tea to his guests but never with saucers, had insurance for divorcers, assurance for enforcers, time for discoursers, lozenges for hoarsers, stirrups for horsers, reins for reinforcers, recourse for coursers, wise words for coarsers, would gobble words with His gob, hobble words with His gait, wobble words with His walk, cobble words on the roadway, bobble words at the circus, nobble words from bank robberies, squabble words at confrontations, Scrabble words at board meetings, burgled swords from the Nobles, escaped to Grenoble, dated a Miss Crayant ignoble, sated a miscreant un-noble, became very ennoble, and settled in a career that was bastardly and dastardly and very decidedly upwardly mobile. He robbed bugles from "The Gables," stole words out of libraries (mediocrity borrows, rabbits burrow, potato farmers wheel-barrow but genius *steals*), got heavenly words from the *Borealis Aurora*, wise words from both Celtic and Delphic *Oracles,* loud words with *His* auricles, aural words from the mountains Ural, Latin words from the Senate Caesural, college words from the sports inter-mural, discounted

19

words from the USAF commissural, medical words inter-
neural, legal words in the jural, painted words on the mural,
took single words from the pleural, farm words from the rural,
un-employed words sinecural, lower extremity words from
the sural, oral words from the sea Aral, visual words from the
retinas of his *retinue*, added words to continue, disconnected
words to discontinue, used healing words for his sinew, and
always commented kindly to an old friend "it's been so long
since I've seen you." He counted revenues on his abacus
in the pupil-count Mount Caucasus under the gray-white
atmosphere *stratocumulus*, "sir, it's us, take us to the circus"
under wispy clouds *cirrus*, "sir, will you rate us" under "halo"
clouds *cirrostratus*, He re-counted avenues on His abaculus
with Papal Count John McCormack under mackerel-blue
skies *cirrocumulus*, calculated obtuse angles in trigonometry
under sunny skies *tumulous*, did calculus very mal-callous
under cloudy skies very *cumulus*, viewed the planets in heaven
imperious in the constellation Sirius right through the high
altocumulus, mapped the heaven's great planets through
the *mammatocumulus*, sang baritone with a soprano under
the gray-blue *altostratus*, ran nimbly under wintry-skies
nimbostratus, hiked straight-laced under the status *stratus*,
and always accumulated columns of heavy, dense clouds very
cumulonimbus.

The Priestly side of Protestant England.

He found the Angelus good for his *animus*, the priests good
for a cuss, a smack in the puss, catholic Angela good for a
buss but *never* a protestant phallus, pious Father Russ with a
wander-truss lust, always raised a damn fuss, always muchafuss
about incubus, blundered on into wonder-truss Gus carrying
his ancient bold blunderbuss onto a cold wanderlust bus, gave
impetus to: There ! A bus; Erebus, there a bus; here a bus,
muchabus; Hark ! A bus, harquebus; thankabus, thank you
very muss; never an omnibus, always a terminus, a succubus
asleep in a recumbentibus, sucking-up to a sleeping trucker-
man incumbent, and a buss on a bus with a pretty girl is just the
ticket. How far, far away or way, way afar would Wells Fargo
go ? Meet Sahib Ram Jam Phull a double-decker conductor
from B'rum, a bakery to a crumb, children out banging a
drum, never in chewing on gum, driving a lent truck in Lent
very hum, in the Borough of Westminster, Kingdom come;
driving *tourista* Edna Lum, a child holding hands with her
mum, the passengers' arses all very numb, a derelict sucking a
plum, an *alky* sipping on rum, a mathematician solving a sum,
a Buddhist rubbing his tum, a baby with a nappied-up bum, a
"babe" with a neat pair, sucking a sweet pear, put all that in
your silly syllabus and drive *that* silly bus ram-jam full. *Ah, me
amor patriae.*

21

Post-pubertal experimentation.

He was a Caledonian saintologist, a conchologist most conical,

a Cameronian runologist, a mythologist most comical, a

Cameroonian rhinologist, a numerologist most chronicle,

a Catonian rheologist, a top-hatted toff most monocle, a

Chelonian pteridologist, a demonologist most euphonical, a

Chthonian psychopathologist, a martyrologist most canonical,

a Ciceronian psychologist, a philologist most architectonical,

He swam naughty and nautilus with a polypus octopus,

discussed phosphorus in the Bosporus with new testament

Leviticus, asked physician Cerberus now can you see us under

the new *caduceus*, drove a Volvo convolvulus, explained

hydrocephalus in a hyperlipidemic hippopotamus with a

ruptured esophagus, manufactured a non-humorous humerus

down-under capturing a polypus platypus, fractured a radius

up-over in the Gloucestershire clover where the cows slip on

cowslips, the dew drops on dewdrops, the love sonnets wear

blue-bonnets, the foxes wear gardening gloves to pick early-

morning handfuls of foxgloves, wear white dinner-gloves for

late-night dancing fox-trots with foxy foxes, there's no ball-room

in the small rooms at the night Ballroom Roxy, don't-knock-

the-rock gnomes like Lichens, the cat caught it's tongue on the

cactus, Fosberg's family made love in the Love grass, the iceberg

lettuce alone say's "let us alone" in the Honeymoon honey-sun, to cut or not to cut the Orcutt grass, that is the answer; is that you ? A-tishoo ! A tissue ! We all fall down; the swine run madly after Schwien Wiener Schnitzle through Schweinitz's sunflowers, you can deal Delia under the asplenium-leaved Diellia, love Lulu in the Lo'ulu *(pritchardia munroi)*, and a Bible Church bell-ringer, a tribal perch hymn-singer, a libel-search binger would never linger to put in and pull out the most livid-wet finger, performed the most cunning cunnilingus (which is always a large plus for tiny ladies with modest busts, a medium plus for huge ladies with rampant busts, a small plus for average ladies with suave busts, a large plus for suave ladies with huge busts, a small plus for huge ladies with modest busts, a medium plus for large ladies with small busts, a huge plus for tiny ladies with average busts, a modest plus for suave ladies with rampant busts, a medium plus for tiny ladies with modest busts, a small plus for suave ladies with average busts, a modest plus for tiny ladies with rampant busts, a huge plus for average ladies with a suave bust, a rampant plus for small ladies with large busts) and whether a nonplus or an overload, an over-plus with a horny toad, overland or down the road, repercuss or temper-goad, boil-pus in acne'd Lew Hoad, much fuss in hackneyed mode, cat-puss or Cyrillic code, wasn't tantamount to Tartarus who came down from Mount Tantalus, paid one denarius for tartar sauce on his road-kill ranunculus, which

23

landed him forever in the soup with the zoot-suit, the Zeus King, the mighty Lord Pegasus. *Tant mieux.*

On Observing Sir Walter Raleigh.

He was a Daltonian phytolithologist, a paleanthropologist most acronycal, a Devonian phraseologist, a hypnologist most antiphonical, a Draconian phonologist, a scientologist most harmonical, in Britain He sang a Neopolitan stanza with Mario Lanza, sang "Santa Lucia" in St. Lucia, in Milan turned a musical bonanza into a cosmopolitan extravaganza, developed schizophrenia in Armenia, asthenia in Parthenia, hypoadrenia in Albania, leukopenia in Lithuania, myasthenia in Malaysia, neurasthenia in Nigeria, oligophrenia in Zambia, phonasthenia in Somalia, presbyophrenia in Russia, psychasthenia in Namibia, catamenia in Colombia, hebephrenia in Croatia, neomenia in Mauritania, sarracenia in Syria and xenophobia in Porto Novo, always helped sister Sister Sinead with her "Sine-Aid" for her sinuses, always greeted girl-friend Meaghan with "hello, it's me again," dated a fine girl in a fine gale who worked for the *Fine Gael,* always pronouncing pronouns naso-palatine and announcing romantic words strictly Valentine, attended orchestral Proms at Royal Albert Hall, mended theatrical props never at all, sold honey from free bees, finagled "free-bees" for "Fingal's Cave," crashed concerts for

"Five Clark Dave," stole "comps" for the romps and pomp-and-circumstance at the palace, denounced rude words from the pimps and Sir *Cum* Stance with malice, and forever took communal bread from His host and communion wine from the chalice. Talk about a fire in the brier, a liar in the briar, the Saints praying, the sinners preying, the thieves prying, and the winding-down winter *wynd* dying. The brief life of John Aubrey in his layered briefs in lawyerly briefs described *"Mary, Countesse of Pembroke, a faire and beautiful Ladie with an excellent witt, a pritty sharpe-ovall face, haire of reddish yellowe, very salacious, and in the Spring of the yeare, when the stallions were to leape the mares, after observing them through a convenient vidette, would act the like sport herselfe most horne with her gallants, notably crooke-back't Cecill, the Earl of Salisbury."* Truly a Joycean nympholepsy, retold many a night by a knight in the Sir Walter Raleigh pub, do drop in at The Dewdrop Inn, then come down to Youghal y'all, and listen carefully. Sir Walter Raleigh, *"getting up one of his Mayds of Honour up against a tree in the wood"* (recounted by Count John Aubrey after having "made" many a maid in *his* honor in the Linden Lea woods) watched as *"the modest mayd (fearful of* her *honour) cryed out to his Honor 'Sir Walter, what doe you me ask; will you undoe me ? Nay, sweet Sir Walter ! Sweet Sir Walter !! Sir Walter !!!'* At last, as the danger and the pleasure

25

grew higher, she cryed out in the extasey 'Swisser Swatter Swisser Swatter.' The mayd proved with child" but Sir Walter never made it to the altar. *Dabis, improbe, poenas.*

Early College Days.

Aaagh, poor, *pauvre,* pontificate Joyce, the rabid Rabbi, the hypochondriacal hydrophobe, the colonic astrophobe, was once bold-told to His face at a fete about His fate, so forever after forgot about laughter, spent time in the rafters contemplating the hereafter, found out that what He was here after was here after He was gone, admired Horace for his *sesquipedalian* polysyllables, never an *antitransubstantiationalist,* always a *floccinaucinihilipilificationist,* studied the *hippopotomonstrosesquipedalianism* of the greater *hepato-cholangio-cholecystosto-cholesterenterostomy* and pre-educated the merry Popes, pre-medicated the mangy pups, premeditated and premedicated with nary-fary, hairy-fairy, rare dairy Queen Mary Poppins on the *supercalifragilisticexpialidociousness* of the far-less messy *laparo-hystero-salpingo-oophorectomy,* of the tar-less *Tobacco Mosaic Virus, Dahlemense Strain,* so after begin the *beguine,* between dear Derreen and the bog-sweating boreen, from the Mountains of Mourne to the boat-bobbing sea, was dejected and infected by a pollysyllabic virus that was a rash to His mustache, put a growth on His stash, gave a weird

26

taste to His potato hash, grew on a football owned by Ferenc
Puskas, and grew a foot and a half long under the microscope:
acetylseryltyosylseryl isoleucylthreonylserylprolylserylgluta
minyl phenyl alanylleucylserylvalyltryptophylalanyl aspartyl
prolylisoleucylglutamylleicyllleucyl asparaginylvalylcysteinyl
threonylseryl serylleucylglycylasparaginylglutaminyl phenyl
alanylglutaminylthreonylglutaminyl glutaminylalanylarginyl
threonylthreonyl glutaminylvalylglutaminylglutaminyl phenyl
alanlylserylglutaminylvalylttry ptophyllysylprolylphenylalanyl
pprolyl glutaminylserylthreonylvalylarginyl phenylalanylproly
lglycylaspartyl valyltyrosyllysylvalvltyrosylarginyltyrosyl aspara
ginylalanylvalylleucylaspartyl prolylleucylisoleucylthreonyl
alanyl leeucylleucylglycylthreonylphenylalanylas partylthreony
larginylasparaginylarginyl isoleucylisoleucylglutamylvalyl
glutamylas paraginylglutaminylglutaminylserylproly lthreonyl
threonylalanylglutamylthreony lleucylaspartylalanylthreony
larginy larginylvalylaspartylaspartylalanyl threonylvalylalany
lisoleucylarginyl serylalanylasparaginylisoleucylas paraginylleu
cylvalylasparaginyl glutamylleucylvalylarginylglycy lthreonylgly
cylleucyltyrosylass paraginylglutaminylasparaginylthreonyl
phenyl alanylglutamylserylmethionylseryl glycylleucylvalyl
tryptophylthreonyl serylalanylprolylalanylserine,
took brazen and bizarre breaths; deep breathing for
prevention, salt inhalations for respiratory retention,

steam inhalations for fixed, draconian measures against
pneumonoultramicroscopicsilicovolcanoconiosis, forever
knowing that he would never know that on August 17th, 2002
at the Summer Commencement of the University of Texas
at Dallas, in the School of Natural Science and Mathematics,
that Jose Juan Gutierrez-Gonzalez was awarded a Ph.D.
for his dissertation : *Synthesis of Diblock, Triblock, and Star*
Copolymers of Poly (2-Dimethyloctylsilyl)-Phenylenevinylene
(DMOS-PPV) and Poly [1-Methoxy-4-(2-Ethylhexyloxy)]-
Phenylenevinylene (MEH-PPV) whilst on January 18th, 2004,
very neat on the internet was an incomplete intercept of
historical and rhetorical, arboricultural and philanthropical,
philosophical and philological, phenomenal and psychological,
pontifical and ministerial dissertations written by twenty
young ten-year olds with bright intellects who dissected the
language, massacred history, fine-lined the time-lines to the
delight and see light, Belo and be light, velcro and bee light,
"hello" and tea light of a tribe with nice features, a scribe on
the bleachers, a bribe of church preachers, a jibe of cheer-
greeters, a vibe of blood-leechers, a Clive of surf creatures,
and the almighty might of Dallas-Fort Worth, Sunday-School
teachers. They were (alleged) to have written that "Egyptian
mummies and their children couldn't live in the Sarah Dessert
as it was too hot and the hot climate forced the inhabitants

to live elsewhere. Their writings were done in hydraulics. The Hebrews made unleavened bread, which is bread made without any ingredients. Moses went up Mount Cyanide for the 10 commandos, but he died before he reached Canada, but the commandos made it. Solomon had 300 wives and 700 porcupines and was a hysterical figure as well as being in the Bible. Without the Greeks there would be no history, except for their young, female, moths (called myths). Socrates gave free advice but his enemies killed him. He later died from an overdose of wedlock, which is very poisonous. After his death, his career went into a dramatic decline. Julius Caesar extinguished himself on the battlefields of Gaul, but was murdered by the Ides of March. Dying, he angrily retorted '*up yours, Brutus*.' Joan of Arc was burnt to a steak. Queen Elizabeth I was a success as the *Virgin Queen* but was very shy. When she exposed herself before her troops they all shouted *hooray !* and that was the end of the fighting for a long while. Gutenberg invented removable type and the Bible. Another important invention at this time was the circulation of the blood. Sir Walter Raleigh invented cigarettes and started smoking. Sir Francis Drake circumcised the world with a 100 foot clipper, which was very dangerous to all his men. William Shakespeare was born in 1564, supposedly on his birthday. He wrote tragedies, comedies and hysterectomies, all in Islamic pentameter. Miguel Cervantes wrote *Donkey Hote*, John Milton wrote *Paradise Lost* but since then no-one has ever found it. Delegates from the 13 aboriginal American States founded the Contented Congress. Thomas Jefferson was a Virgin and with Benjamin Franklin were two of the original singers of the Declaration of Independence and declared *a horse divided against itself cannot stand*. Abraham Lincoln was America's greatest Precedent. His mother died in infancy, and he was born in a log cabin which he built with his own hands. He freed the slaves by signing the Emasculation Proclamation. On April 14, 1865, Lincoln was shot by John Wilkes Booth, an actor in a moving picture show. This ruined Booth's career. Johann Bach wrote many compositions and had many children. In between he practiced on an old spinster which he kept in the attic. Bach died from 1750 to the present. Handel was very large, being one half German, one half Italian and one half English. Beethoven was deaf so he wrote very loud music and was the father of Rock and Roll. He took long walks in the forest, even though his parents were always calling him. He expired in 1827 and eventually died from this. The nineteenth century was a time of inventions when people stopped reproducing by hand and started reproducing with machines. The invention of the steamboat caused a network of rivers to spring up. Cyrus McCormick invented the McCormick raper, which did the work of a 100 men. Louis Pasteur discovered a cure for rabbits. Charles Darwin wrote the *Organ of Species* and said God's days were not just 24 hours, but without watches nobody knew. Madman Curie discovered radio, so other women scientists didn't get to find radios as they were already taken. Karl Marx was one of the Marx brothers. The other 3 were in movies but Karl made speeches and started revolutions." *Mutatis mutandis.*

Bach in Two Minuets.

But then again, never had so much of Wolfgang Amadeus Mozart's brilliant, rutilant, aureate, lambent, fulgent, effulgent, refulgent, relucent, coruscating, fulgid, adroit, percipient, perspicacious, sagacious, sapient, erudite, *bravura* ever been employed to give the appearance of such a fatuitous, insensate and incogitant *Allegro*; such an addlepated, mulish and obdurate *Menuetto: Maestoso*; such a fatuous, *doiled*, *glaikit* and vapid *Adagio cantabile*; cumulating in a risible and anserine *Presto*, of such puerile stupidity as in *The Musical Joke.* Brahms was up in arms *nobilmente,* Beethoven was awash in charms *teneramente,* Mendel's Son set his night-time alarms *dolente,* Rimsky-Korsakov stayed the course *piacevole,* leaving Benjamin Britten to be smitten by Britain's Big Ben *grave.* Saint-Saens read *affrettando*, Debussey bled

31

tempo primo, Bach was abed *pizzicato*, Schubert was shoeless *staccato*, Dvorak was voraciously *animato*, Sibelius dated Sybil a*ppassionato*, Elgar was never in Rathgar *ma non troppo*, Grieg was aggregious *parlante*, Tchaikovsky was sky-high *lontano*, Pagganini was in Calabria *lusingando*, Vivaldi was always lively *suave*, whilst Gustav Holst (and this author) were both English Gentlemen born in the borough of Cheltenham *most thorough*. At least the majority opinion of the minority pinions of the *antidisestablishmentarianists* with or without Sir Winston Churchill, Mark Twain and George Bernard Shaw was that Wagner's music was always much better than what it sounded. *Adagio, mancando, morendo, slargando, to smorzando.*

Playing Yippee, Yi, Yo with the YUPPIES.

He visualized anthroscopy with *burnt out but opulent* BOBO's, pilloried bletonism with *black, urban, professional* BUPPIE's; was a Captain with Nancy who petitioned capnomancy with *dual income, no kid* DINKIE's; argued augury with *dual income, no kids* (yet) DINKY's; practised pyromancy with *destitute, unemployed, mature, professional* DUMP's; was beneath belomancy with *golden oldies, live dangerously* GOLDIE's; took a fancy to Nancy but not leconomancy with *gay, urban professional* GUPPIE's, sprayed hairspray most dicey for haruspicy with *lots of money but a real dickhead* LOMBARD's; tried scientific romancy without sciomancy with *not in my backyard* NIMBY's; no spodomancy with *one income, no kid* OINK's; was chancey with osteomancy with *persons inheriting parents' property* PIPPIE's; became algebraic and arithmancy with *poncy, urban, professional* PUPPIE's; preached bibliomancy with *self-centered, urban male* SCUM; scoped Gyros in Greece but despised gyromancy with *single income, loads of kids* SILKY's; wielded his peg-leg, his pinion (but never an opinion) despite pegomancy with *single income, no boyfriend, absolutely desperate* SINBAD's; would birdwatch and watch birds with aornithomancy with *single, independent, no kid* SINK's; played Florence Nightingale with lampadomancy with *single income, two kids, outrageous mortgage* SITCOM's; siphoned cider with sideromancy with *well-off, older person* WOOPIE's; was optimistic with pessomancy with *young, affluent parent* YAPPIE's; and inevitably sorted-out sortilege, geloscopy and hieroscopia with *young, urban, professional person* YUPPIES.

Experiences with Enslaved Bricklayers.

He discussed masonry freely with political adversaries, pantisocracy with Sovereign Grand Inspector Generals, militocracy with Sublime Princes of the Royal Secret, exarchy with Grand Inspector Inquisitor Commanders, bureaucracy with Knights of the Black and White Eagles, ecclesiarchy with Grand Elected Knights Kadosh, gerontocracy with Knights of Saint Andrew, patriarchy with Knight of the Sun, Prince Adepts; kritarchy with Grand Commanders of the Temple, androcacy with Princes of Mercy, aristocracy with Chevaliers of the Brazen Serpent, autocracy with Princes of the Tabernacle, democracy with Chiefs of the Tabernacle, ptochocracy with Princes of Libanus, Royal Hatchet; paparchy with Patriachs Noachite, Prussians Chevalier; timocracy with Venerable Grand Masters, theocracy with Grand Pontiffs, hagiarchy with Knights of the Eagle & Pelican and Sovereign Princes Rose Croix of Heredom, doulocracy with Knights of the East and West, oligarchy with the Princes of Jer-*USA*-lem, technocracy with the Knights of the Sword & of the East, plutocracy with the Scottish Knights of Perfection, gynarchy with the Royal Arc of Enoch, kakistocracy with the Grand Master Architect, cottonocracy with the Sublime Knights, Chevalier Elects; pantisocracy with Illustrious Masters Elect of Fifteen, theocrasy with the Superintendents of the Building, timocracy with the Provosts and Judges, viewed the Intimate Secretary most binocular, joked with the Perfect Master most jocular, relocated with the Secret Master most locular, reviewed the Master Mason most monocular, heard the Fellow Craft most auricular and held a most enlightening conversation with the Entered Apprentice most vocular. *In vino veritas.*

Preventive Medicine.

Araagh, revert forwards to our own Hero, a genuine Greek-seeking, ear-tweaking gynotikolobomassophile, His fears verily would vacillate, His right ear would osculate, His wrong ear would oscillate, His nose would fumigate and His tongue would articulate, His height would abbreviate, His throne he would abdicate, His upper abdomen abdicate, His belly-button abominate, His lower abdomen predominate, His gait would accelerate, His accent accentuate, His thyroid would acclimate, His lungs would hyper-inflate, His bronchioles would happily aerate, His pancreas would unhappily acetate, His lymph glands would activate, His brain would acuminate, His mind would adjudicate, His loins would adulterate, His fingers would agitate, His bronchi would alveolate, His feet would ambulate, His elbows would angulate, His speech would animate, His words would annotate, His expectancy would anticipate, His prostate became apostolate, His arms would arbitrate, His glottis would aspirate, His larynx asphyxiate, His knowledge assimilate, His feelings attenuate, His reason authenticate, His sacrum would bifurcate, His brain hemispheres would bilobulate, His eyes would binoculate, His ears would bipinnate, His triceps would bimusculate, His calcaneum would calumniate, His breathing would camphorate, His cranium would capitate, His knee joints encapsulate, His drinks He would carbonate, His food He would masticate, His ear-wax would caseate, His thinking would cerebrate, His Ampulla of Vater would circinate, His arterio-venous would circulate, His red blood cells corpusculate, His love-life would celibate, His movements circumambulate, His voyages circumnavigate, His balance cochleate, His attitude cogitate, His sweat would condensate, His lies He would confabulate, His vision conjugate, His rectum would constipate, His genitals would copulate, His penis ejaculate, His soft tissues emaciate, His radiance emanate, His hormones emasculate, His arguments corticate, His ashes cremate, His coffee He would decaffeinate, His anus would defecate, His head-hair would defoliate, His joints would degenerate, His esophagus deglutinate, His body-water would dehydrate, His tooth-enamel would dentate, His semen would germinate and then delightfully despumate, His appendages would desquamate, His liver would detoxicate, His strabismus would deviate, His Doctor would diagnosticate, His Seer would prognosticate, His appearance would dilapidate, His pupils dilate, His wrist joint disarticulate, His chest-hair would depilate, His shoulder would dislocate, when toothless was edentate, His pharynx would eructate, His bowels would

36

evacuate, His bladder would urinate, His heart beating fibrillate when relate of His one sexual fate on a terrible 1896 date when given the green light at dear Dublin's near red-light rear gate. His diaphoresis would evaporate, His Guinness would inebriate, His small bowel would eviscerate, His thought processes excogitate, His skin would excoriate, when upset He would salivate, His armpits would sanitate, His appetite satiate, His manner sedate, His tight collar most strangulate, His pillow most suffocate, His sleep very supinate, His knee ligaments excruciate, His sputum expectorate, His urine extravasate, His ear-drums would fenestrate, His tooth-paste He would fluoridate, His vitamins He would foliate, without a wife He would fornicate, on His own He would masturbate, His medicines he would medicate, whether salicylate or opiate, His ego would self-inflate, His cigarettes infumate, His manners infuriate, His vaccines inoculate, His appetite insatiate, His after-dinner speeches intonate, His stomach quite ulcerate, He ate for His ideal weight, His wealth He would circumstantiate, His friends he would celebrate, His enemies He would castigate, His audience He would captivate, yet would spend His quiet time most consumate and His diet time most ruminate in the thick of the thicket around a thatched cottage quite rusticate. He would sing borborygmi to an African pigmy, light up His epicondylitis at tennis, tear up His uvula at the opera, stamp out His tinea pedis, purse His philtrum at Phil, race His pulse tachycardia, bursae on His knees while talking to housemaids, squint strabismus, watched long-distances myopic, matched short distances presbyopic, cried onions over His bunions, and was always stern and would learn with His own xiphisternum. Throughout the Nation, NEVER did it with Jason, not even a Mason, much less at a station, but always with elation, and without hesitation, when the feeling was right, and being uptight, after a suppertime bite, would give himself a fright, and from a considerable height, without any light, and with all his might, and always out of sight, would delight in the practice of self-fornication. This little book is green, orange and white and yet is read all over, yet crustacean critics, the Publisher, the Priestly castes and sterilizing baths, and even Dr. Spurgeon, the surgeon, all completely failed to remove it's appendix. *Medicinae Doctorem !*

Always the Sesquipedalian Irishman, the Epicurean Connoisseur.

He was a true autarchic author-chic, always asleep for a Wake, awake for a dream, bespoke very clean, always generous never mean, had pragmatism and astigmatism, a cornucopia with myopia, a Deuteronomy with deuteranopia, never a Ministerian with ever-present presbyopia but always a Presbyterian with the never-absent sherry, He pervertedly observed sex-therapists septuagenarian thumb-swallow hors d'oevres, speech-wallowed with six Baptist veterinarians about horses ovaries, and with equestrian fright and Epicurean delight in front of the Papists did fine, and did finessedly, finger-eat, fine-dine, fine-wine, with sartorial splendour, consummate ease, was dicey with peas, picked a fine time with Warren and Jimmy to *dine Buffet*, brought the Muppets, Little Miss Muppet, to sup-it on tuppets, had no way with curds but convinced hungry Kurds, made the English eat their words, the Welsh take a leak, the Scots sip a scotch, the Isle of Mann women to manage their manners, the Cornish to eat hen, the Isle O'Wighters to jettison their lighters, corral their fighters, and as pigs love their truffles, He soothed his ruffles, packed his bags-duffle, and sat down to eat on a tableau most neat *lopadotemachosselachogaleo kranioleipsanodrimhypotrimmatosilphio paraomelitokatakechy menokchlepikossypho phattopcristeralektryonoptekephalliokig klopeleiolagoiosiraiobaphetraganopterygon* off a dainty, delightful deli-plate dish with Aristophanes. Otherwise it was Anatole's *Veloute aux fleurs de courgette*, Bertie Wooster's *Sylphides a la creme d'Ecrivisses*, Tom Travers' *Mignonette de poulet de petit duc*, Dahlia Travers' *Niege aux perles des Alpes*, Jeeves' *Timbale de ris de veau Toulousaine*, leaving the *Points d'asperges a la Mistinguette* for Wodehouse himself. Joyce-Man was never suspicious (liked the *Nonettes de poulet Agnes Sorel*) and was ever avaricious (spiked the *Benedictins Blancs*), started out with a wide grin (hiked the *Selle d'Agneau aux laitures a la Grecque*) and ended up with a most narrow chagrin (biked *Diablotins*) in the mire and (Nike'd the *Caviar Frais*) out of the fire with the true writers and un-true liars, soloists and choirs, briars and briers, washers and driers, City laughers and Town Criers, clarifiers and classifiers, sellers and buyers, vilifiers and vivifiers, black Friars and white liars, Mayers and Meiers and Meyers and Myers, appliers and amplifiers, codifers and compliers, purifiers and putrifiers, verifiers and versifiers, ratifiers and rectifiers, reliers and repliers, notifiers and nullifiers, modifiers and mollifiers, testifiers and terrifiers, sanctifiers and satisfiers, glorifiers and gratifiers, signifiers and simplifiers, stupefiers and suppliers, disqualifiers and diversifiers, falsifiers and fortifiers, electrifiers and exempifers, identifiers and impliers, electrifiers and exemplifiers, mortifiers and multipliers, personifiers and petrifiers, liquifiers and magnifiers, indemnifiers and intensifiers, all armed with the pliers to break in the tires and break out the cases of the Biedermeier beer. *Pax vobiscum.*

On Meeting William Webb Ellis.

He scrummed-down in winter-shorts and sprang up on the tennis courts for the Summer lure of the Springboks, He drummed-up support and crumbed-down with consorts for the

Winter tour of the "All Blacks," He strummed in the twilight against the guile of the "Black Caps," His gated ancestors raining pots and pans on the heads and hats of the hated "Black and Tans," He drum-called and wall-clocked the British Lions through the gales, had impatience with Patience but never with His Hispanic panicked patients, impatiently took Patience to Rugby for play sense at Six Nations Rugby, hurled barley at the Harlequins for barely try-ing, left the "off License", climbed a fence without a licence, then took offence against the London Irish for playing Englishmen, took the wind out of the sails of the wassailing Wallabees, hailed the Welsh Dragons through the hail, railed at the Scots on the sleeper-full *Flying Scotsman* o'er the creeper-full rails, wagged his orchestrating finger through the torque-freighting rails at rich Richard Wagner who failed to attend the *Flying Dutchman*, watched Ireland versus France, it really wasn't much, man; saw the English full-back reluctantly kick the ball at a "butch" man, saved up for the Italian tour of the Hellenes, accompanied Lemuel Gulliver to watch golfing Lilly putt in Lilliput, heard Bob Robding nag his wife in Brobdingnag, had a lap-dance with Uta in Laputa, had a shave in balmy Balnibarbi, lugged his luggage to Luggnagg (with Bob Robding's wife nagging poor Bob while he was lugging *her* luggage), had a rub-a-dub-dub in a glub-a-dub-tub in Glubbdubdrib, landed in the Land of the Rising Sun after dark in Japan, left the Ireland of the Houlihans for the dire Land of the Houyhnhnms, went roaming-in-the-gloaming, but never laughed so much as when climbing Llareggub Hill all-the-while listening to the glistening Tylan Dhomas describe the unshaved, nicotine-stained, egg-yellowed, saliva-encrusted, leek-souped, coryza-matted, weeping-walrus mustachioed old Mr Pugh secretly reading from *Lives of the Great Poisoners.* He then took honey from honey-bees, made money at spelling bee's, chased away all the bumblebees, himself *The Man* at tea watching many manatees and clocking zany "wanna-be's," catching disparate Chelsea Pensioners, duplicate oversea tensioners and desperate "make-a-plea" abstentioners, delightedly and politely, delightfully and politefully dispensing "mind-your-manners-please" entreaties while simultaneously hatching diabolical *diaspora* humanities. And never picked up the circular football at Rugby and ran off with it. *Lese majeste.*

On Moving to Trieste.

He went lighting the Wolfe bonfires of the Tom "Fu Chu Man" vanities, delighting Capote *in lieu* of the "True Man" profundities, fighting my pal Al Capone over Big Louie's "Hit Man" profanities, dining on shrimps and anemones and wining on fine Burgundies, dispensed Hail ! Hearty ! and genuine *bon hommie's;* went high-lighting the guardians

of the Bedlam insanities, hand-fighting with the wardens
of the London Zoo epiphanies, getting Al Gored by the
democratic gorillas, amBushed by the Republican flotillas,
you can watch the chimps change by stealing the chump-
change thrown at fanatic chimpanzees, is a catastrophe with
chickadees, becomes hysterical with the Communist Chinese
but hymnal with the Christmas trees, never dated Cherokees
but attended tribal jamborees, had admirers and loyal
devotees, accumulated Belvedere diplomas and distinguished
UCD degrees, enjoyed daytime travel and the duty-frees,
hated the Scottish highlands with their daily freeze, enjoyed
Irish whisky and French *eau-de-vie's*, has conversations
with the leprechaun's and sugar-plum fairies, lost his frisbee
in the evergreen trees, ate fricassee with the Japanese,
spoke Arabic with the Lebanese, sang the *Marseillaise* in
the Marshalseas, named the McFees, the McGees and the
McKees as mortgagees, observed new comets midst the
nebulae, dated Rosalies and Penelopes with Ph.D.'s, phoned
Pharisees and seduced Sadducees, cooked recipes, combed
pedigrees, percolated vegetables and circulated potpourris,
went from Sault St. Marie to Tennessee without getting
travelers checks with guarantees, shouted stunning *Reparti's*
at dumb football referees, always reciting the poetic lines
of the Irish saloon writers at Pub Hannaty's, twilighting

the British ladies at late-afternoon Hannah's teas, inciting reason in the American medical profession with Dr Hanna and the MRCP's, indicting treason in the Canadian legal profession with Nelson Eddy and the RCMP's, re-lighting the embers of Scotland's Robbie Burns in the poem-strewn Hebrides, was impressed by the biting of African Baboons in the Savannah trees, was distressed by the kiting of the North Perth aborigines, was compressed by the bureaucratese of the Western Academies, left His best writing anonymous on the walls of the Central Park lavatories, translated the analyses of the Maimonides antitheses, spoke computerese to the Annamese, ran out of anti-freeze, gave frozen peas to the Viennese, could never appease the arrogant Aragonese, the kayaking Arakanese, the assuming Assamese; built non-windy vortices for the wine-drinking Veronese, quilt fine windy voyages for the main-sailing Portuguese, lit orchestral fires for the sabbatical choirs in the Pyrenees, put out funeral pyres for the dramatical Squires amongst the British Ceylonese, raised schooner-full buyers for the gold-trading Pirate-sleaze, praised lunar-full electricity to the wandering Senegalese, sailed the breeze in Belize, was bee's knees with the Bengalese, ate bologna sausages in Bologna with the Bolognese, ate Swiss cheese and small apples to the tease of the "Big Apple" Brooklynese, was always at

44

ease in Manhattan speaking New Yorkese, rode bucking

broncs in the Bronx on New Year's Eve, in Hong Kong spoke

Cantonese, spoke daring Mandarin with a grin to a curious

man in distant Manchuria, spoke Malayalam in Dar-Es-

Salaam, spoke Maltese to Mephistopheles, Nepalese to the

Milanese, Navarrese to Louise and Leonese, Johnsonese

to the Javanese, addressed Okinawa poets in journalese,

in Shanghai the ducks speak Pekinese, in Thailand the

cats speak Siamese, don't mention the God-Father to the

Genovese, at the Pentagon its Pentagonese, try discussing

the Pleiades with Pierides in the Hesperides, hypotheses

with Eumenides in Caryatides, parentheses with Hercules,

talking Singhalese with Socrates, creating syntheses with

the Havanese, playing polonaises with the *Polonese,* flying

trapeze with the Tyrolese, smelting lead with the Burmese,

breaking heads with the "Moonies" in the petal-strewn

boonies, bleeding hearts with the liberals in Dettol-ruined

Carlylese, wearing an "over-the-head" chemise to the chemist

very Sudanese, then settled down with a sigh by the side of the

Zuyder Zee, had a tryst with Nora, a fauna explora, and then

watched the tear-weeping, willow-wood, grow tall and free;

the sheer creeping, pillar-wood consumed by the sap-seeping

wattle-trees; surrounded by whopping-whale whiffletrees and

the whale-of-a gale wail as the tail of the wind wanders cursing and coursing through the wind-whipping whipple-trees. *Faute de mieux*.

Mundane Middle Age.

He became a bread-and-jam butterer, a butterfly flutterer, a Mongoloid mutterer, a saliva-spitting splutterer, a diesel engine sputterer, a tongue-twisting stutterer, and a eloquent utterer; made waistcoats more buttony, satiated His gluttony, ate roast lamb most muttony, made shoes freebootery, canned peaches fruitery, polished up pewtery and chopped down trees rootery; made His feet more immovable, His logic more improvable, His furniture irremovable, his sentences more movable, His sonnets more provable, His appendix removable, His reproach more approvable and His approach more reprovable. He played chess with a *Bad Bishop*, tried *Rank*, *Pin* and *Promotion*, played *Sans Voir* with the Germans, *J'Adoube* with the Austrians, *Zugzwang* with the Chinese, *Zwischenzug* with the Swiss, passed the Austrians *En Passant*, surprise everyone *En Prise* with the enterprising N. Ter Prize, Esq., ordered triple prawns (with a *Skewer*) and got *Doubled Pawns*, they refused a *Perpetual Check*, He pulled out a *Buried Piece*, and when the *Discovered Check* was found in the *Castle* beside the *Base of Pawn Chain*, His *Sacrifice* was nice, *File* was dead *Center*, late *Development* got a *Promotion*, the *Skewer* was *Diagonal*, and He ended up a *Stalemate* with a plate of stale meat with His best mates, Mate. He bespoke editors distrustfully, lovers most lustfully, treated many a mistress in distress most mistrustfully but pressed the Irish Guards in full dress most lustfully; Say Hello ! And Good Morrow ! to the PPO dog-and-pony show, where your money they'll borrow, you'll be full of sorrow, here-today, gone-tomorrow, it's a daytime nightmare and a night-time horror, betcha can't get HMO Aetna to say "I'm real glad I met ya" and get *them* to pay for your "cold Sicilian slumber" while you stayed in Palermo with a "hot little number," and when the boiling pot simmered-down be ready to "sup-up" and shut up, sum-up your lava-stories and gum-up your lavatories, before elegantly plummeting down the slope and elephantly trumpeting up the summit of the Mediterranean's subterranean Mount Etna ! Now strange as it seems, He ate re-fried beans with condemned writers and chased runner-beans with "has-been" blighters, drank deuterium with delirium, radium in the Stadium, vanadium at the Velodrome, palladium at the Palladium, tried pallium for palliation, thallium for titilation, tried not to be trashed by the critic Jill Kneerim (even though all *His* true friends would never let *her* get anywhere near Him) as He knew she would bash Him and trash Him, cash-in on Him and thresh Him, crash Him and dash Him, diss Him and fashion Him, gash Him and hash Him, lash Him and mash Him, gnash Him and squash Him, rash Him and stash Him, sash Him and wreck Him and would dump

47

Him and pump Him, bump Him and clump Him, hump Him and jump Him, lump Him and mumps Him, rump Him and stump Him, Donald and trump Him, whup Him and whip Him until He started-down and ended-up, topped-up and bottom-down, inside the sleazy and slush-full, breezy and bush-full, easy and crush-full, greasy and hush-full, measly and mush-full, queasy and tush-full, weasely and shush-full South Boston trash-cans. He then entered competition "must-wins," plied His trade in the shade and tried to get paid, traded His pliers for jade with a transaction made, lied shady to Lady O'Grady to get gravy-grave laid, pounded the pavements for a few shekels made, swore on the Bible, forewent His libel, unearthed His baptismal font just to get "saved" by the Evangelists before His pure writing-lust turned to more lightning-dust in the Hill and Barlow down-and-dirty, beetroot red, asparagus dread, cauliflower bread, Brussels sprouts, Belgian cabbages, sold-out celery, dead-space pretty miss misplanted eggplants, deadbeat-author dustbins. *Totius vobis frontem tabernae sopionibus scribam.*

Medical School Acceptance (Short James in Long Johns).

From proctorship to doctorship before His proctor ever told Him what being a young *Doktor* meant, even when his distinguished white coat he lent, he was opined that coughs and sneezes would spread all diseases, was intimidated by wheezes, pollen spread on the breezes, patients get cold when it freezes, herbal medicine appeases but sometimes gives you the queezes, the nurses are teases, and He had to put up with the injustice of dear Dr Justice who was inclined to repeat at least three times a week that common diagnoses were common, uncommon diagnoses were uncommon, that uncommon presentations of common diagnoses were far more common than uncommon diagnoses. Ring-a-ring-a-roses we all fall down. So most good judgement must come from bad experience and most of that would have to come from bad judgement. But the good-as-gold Joyce, in His trembling voice, professed to his Professor, the ultimate Confessor, He was not James the lesser, but Joyce (who was better), and had stuffed all His medical books back in the dresser. Before criticising anyone He would walk a mile in their shoes, get a skinful of booze, he had nothing to lose, got drunk with Conor Cruise, figured out a ruse, and ended a mile away at His house with a new pair of shoes. Now having met chamber-maid Nora, and having fancied her *flora*, He was rendered muted by Cupid and felt He was never too old to learn something stupid. He watched in awe at the ambuscade patience for ambulatory patients of the ambient ambulance men on their well-balanced monuments, yet sat in the basement with young Roger Casement, between them they could never figure out what a medical case meant, they sat on the pavement, picked at the cement, they *knew* what nurse Maeve meant, but *not* what Doctor Dave meant, but went into the tent, roared their lungs at full vent, and choired "Doctors differ and patients die, 'Tis not the life for you and I." They used to be indecisive but now they weren't sure. "I always take life with a grain of salt" said Casement, to which Joyce added "plus a slice of lemon and a shot of Tequila." *Nostalgia isn't what it used to be.*

The Rain in Ireland falls mainly on the Unprotected Mane.

Having been born in Ireland he was no ombrophobic. To His lightning-lit wonderment He found out where the white lightning went and what the black thunder meant, He never figured out where His keraunophobia went, His disencumber meant slumber, His dismember sent humbler, the members drank tumblers, the Mummers became fumblers, the robbers became bunglers, the embers were dying, the elders were lying but at long-last in a short-fast His parents finally convinced Him that "Thunder-Land" was in Walt Disney-Land, that not only upside-down Alice but *real* fairies lived in Wonderland, that male "fairies" lived in Never-Land, and *always* warned Him to "never-ever leave your pack, son" around Michael Jackson. The geography of Ireland was that it was surrounded by water and had land in the middle. But what *really* winced Him was that He had traveled overland through Ireland, through yonder-land with his *Ceili* band, o'er the *wather* to Sunderland, so He stood up and stomped out and stormed over to Stormont where the all-at-once rain ante-diluvial made Him feel like a dunce home-alone again cartographical, the seeping rain microscopical was wet-weeping on the closed window pane topographical, the dry, creeping train characteristical was debt-weeping and wet-keeping his seeping-wound pain expurgatorial; the cold, whetting rain insurrectional to His thighs incorporeal brought hot wetting tears to His eyes theosophical; the tearing rain "on-the-fly" tearing a hole in His fly horological, the over-the-weir rain photographical started Him wearying again theological, the acid rain undeniable wore a hole in John Constable's *Hay Wain* most friable, the pouring rain in every pore made A. N. Other English Constable's poor skin very sore and cry-able, the Queen's reign made the Police Constable's dour shin very more fortifiable, pouring whisky in His water in a gin-joint numbed His joint pain forever more pliable, the bog-misting rain obscured the terrain down the fog-glistening lane petrifiable, the campaign champagne was maintained and left chained at Charles's Wain quantifiable by the chamberlain in Champlain most qualifiable, wrapped His plane cell-o-phone in plain cellophane just as His aero-plane invaluable had to hydroplane acidifiable through a hurricane magnifiable, caught an aquaplane inflammable from Cockaigne respectable, hijacked by the *Sinn Fein* most deniable, ate *chow mein* in a pursuit plane incomparable from the *mid-mediterrane* interchangeable to Bahrain justifiable, rode and ho'd on a pleasure train impregnable with a coxswain laudable from Maine placable to Ukraine unmatchable, lode a battering ram with a nattering man onto a clattering train ineffaceable, departing simmering Spain unmatchable for the shimmering Seine presentable, boat-rowed with a boatswain adorable from Aisne acceptable to the Bayne diversifiable, got chilblains reliable while waiting to see whether whooping cranes would alight on the wood-iced, snow-spliced, fog-shrouded weather vanes rarefiable; got lukewarm pains incurable from waiting for Apostle Luke most abstain undeniable, was able to pick sugar-cane with Abel and Cain in the evening in the Eden of gardens plain pacifiable, no snoring in the mornings on the cold Des Moines plains exemplifiable, forgot about Great Britain's always-talking Michael Caine satisfiable, always seen walking with the great Caine's Great Danes vitrifiable, it's ideally non-fictional to "Remember the Maine" classifiable, and non ideally most fictional to forget the "Mutiny on the Caine" most phantasmagorial. *Regime ancien.*

Bob Dylan the Villian and Sweet Baby Jane.

The "great-white" Joyce-write would now abstain undeniable,
ingrain again defiable, arraign most appliable, attain verifiable,
atwain rectifiable, appertain falsifiable, joined in the brain-drain
solidifiable, wrote deraign most reliable with His forebrain
electrifiable, would remain with His mid-brain compliable,
disdain liquefiable, with His hind-brain reliable, His lame-
brain impliable would feelings constrain saponifiable, lost
objects claimed very viable, His ideas waned very triable,
His appearance vain and very bribable, from lodgings
urbane indescribable, bridle reins un-reined in a manner
most scribable, her bridal trains restrained very describable,
Monarchs un-reign with heretics scribing at Scrabble, His
scatterbrain inscribable would down-size and up-stage Mark
Twain monetarily subscribable, would downgrade a swain
imbibable, upgrade the terrain very dividable, utter profane
verifiable, Kings pre-ordain monomaniacal, Bishops co-ordain
demoniacal, against discomforts complain hypochondriacal,
His featherbrain encyclopediacal would His lifestyle maintain
paradisiacal, contain counterpanes Zodiacal, prisoners
detain maniacal, passengers detrain elegiacal, idiots entertain
simoniacal, teachers ingrain bibliomaniacal, patients insane
cardiacal, ideas inane prosodiacal, inter-marriages inter-reign
with compliancy, Lady McLaine would fritter Frito-Lay potato

chips in her domestic domain most bestridable, Lady McLayne
would ward off Ward Lay with incredible disdain elegiacal,
but Joyce the juice-man would lay Lady Jane in the lane very
pliantly, lay pre-paid Lady Elaine when in conjugal pain most
reliantly, but not even Bob Dylan could lay vain Lady Jayne
upon *her* big, brass, bed. *Salem ac leporem.*

Pre-Pubertal Misgivings.

Whether the skein and soutane, frangipane and suzerain,
moraine and mortmain, fine and mis-feign, sprain and
sextain, would any layman lay any gay woman, would any
gay man lay a layman, would any gay-woman lay any gay
man, would any gay woman lay the Babylonian table, would
any May bride deride her lay husband, from bored dildo's
in bordello's, from the rich houses to the ditch hovels, from
the poor spouses to the rich Ivor Novello, from Boccaccio's
Decameron novella to a nine-day novena, a novitiate Novi
Sad *novillero* this way and thither, no way nowhither,
which witch would grovel in the gravel beneath the grave
gallows, they swallow cooked swallows in mid-night rituals
in pitch-black Creepy Hollow, it's hemlock and locked hems
in harems to wallow, for a piece of the action you just say
"hello," it's shirt-opened up-fronts as affronts to follow, from
the "open houses" for sale to closed blouses retail, from

cool swan-necks at Coole to the long-necked O'Doul's, from the new naval fools with old Natal Province ghouls, from ante-natal spasmodics to Labor and Delivery tools, from Auntie's navel sweating to Uncle Pavel's rules, perchance to marinate with mariners in Neville Mariner's schemes, Dylan Thomas and Captain Kat wrestling mermaids in their dreams, it's navels in post-natal for new babies drool, new novel Navy women dress fashionably "cool," old jovial Navy men read new novels at finishing school, it's school fees up the navels, from the "open houses" to the gardening gavels, from "Brideshead Revisited" to "Gulliver's Travels," our faltering memories remain and retain, restrain and regain, pertain and enchain, arraign and unchain, demure and demimondaine, germane and humane, fain would I explain, it's all washing-up water flushed down the drain. *Lasciva est nobis paginas vita proba.*

The Prodigal's Return to Auld Eireann (Part the First).

He got His polyglot *Clan na nGael* clan in a gale in the "Golden Vale" of Tipperary where the clans are quite varied, the rain reigns contrary, the mountains are scary, the locals wear bi-focals and tell tall tale-stories about lively, lovely, lovingly little *leprechauns*, band-shy banned *banshees* and the charming, chateau-on-a-plateau *chatelain* fairies. (Just can't compare in Kildare to make "Tippecanoe" William Henry Harrison shiver as he tipped his canoe in the Tippecanoe River, before he became "dead-meat and fresh-liver" to Tecumseh's butchers). He got the *Cuman na mBan* women to Celter-shelter "come on in ma van," the *Cumann na nGaedheal* to Hell-or-to-skelter "come on now you glad heels," and made Him very wistful and list-full, mist-full and pissed-full, wish-full and kiss-full to see His dear old mother in near and dear auld Ireland again. He observed Leopold Bloom observing the O'Connell Street trolley in the window reflections without genuflections and eating confections to make instantaneous deflections of spontaneous connections between the loud trolley departing and Bloom's loud folly of farting ! Dr Papyrus played the *Londonderry Aire*, Dr Plume loved the London Ferry air, Dr Chapter paid the London to Derry fare, Dr Verse attended the merry *Scarborough Faire*, but only queer and dear Dr Flatus knew when that Spring-like air would come blowing out through our dear friend Bloom's fine *derriere !* Window shopping in Dublin window-named and window-framed the Offices of Dewy, Cheatem and Howe (and how !) Financiers; U. Hurryem, W. E. Buryem (like now !) Morticians; Findem, Feelem, Fuckum and Forgetem (that's wow !) Gentlemen's Club; Doctor Quiet and Doctor Diet (Holy Cow !) Preventive Medicine; Bashem, Trashem and Countemout (Biff, Pow !)

Boxing Gym; U. Sow and W. E. Reap (and sow !) Farmer's Guild; Will Pontificate, Wile U. Vacillate (and row !) Divorce Lawyers; Will Legislate, A. Magistrate and I. Judge (and vow !) Marriage Licences; Goldblum and Silverman, (made silk purses out of ears sow !) JEWelers; Al Wheys A. Poorman, (plunk money down now !) Junk Bronzes; and always for lost keys, The Brass MonKEY, Locksmiths. "Hey, Hey, we're the Monkies, running around; Hay, Hay, where's my brass keys, they fell on the ground." He kept on His stockings to survive the lightning most shocking, walked a mile is *His* moccasins to Penzance as penance for His mocking sins, traveled to Manassas to escape His assassins, left dear auld Dublin to go "Beyond the Pale," cost Him a right arm and a left leg to leave Armagh to go *even further* beyond that Pale to carry this pail with His left arm in a sling, Him an outcast with His left leg in the right cast, He left his right tribe in the wrong caste, His dexiotrophic Father left (which was wrong) which left his wronged (yes ! that's right) laeotropic Mother aghast, brother Dexter was very sinister, sister Sinister was ambidextrous, his *die* had been cast, he'd been on a fast, his fame he would soon out-present despite rumours from his late inside-out past, his "baby-boomer" schooner wood out-mast the Oklahoma "Sooner" schooner but not out-last the Bing Crosby "swooner" crooner and with the set of His sails and not the whim of the gales, at a "whale of a sale" let out a wail, put a sail on a whale, and then had a whale of a sail on the ocean seas vast. *Chacun a son gout.*

Mid-Life Crisis.

With over one foot of soot on His well under-foot boots and with underhand loot in his over-all suit, he went clearing out enemies from the Struma to the Duma, clean-sweeping out chimneys from Bimini to Rhiminy, grieving a broken-hearts trail in the Heart of Midlothian, heaving a hearth-full of shale in the "Mucky Duck" Midlands, went balancing the despondency of the defoliation of the throng-full bushes with the respondency of the despoliation of the song-full thrushes, started re-mapping the subterranean dermaptirans, re-started mopping up the over-terrainean dermopterans, went keel-hauling the malcontents from the also-rans, steal-hauling the steel from the moving vans, hauling a heart-full of hope in the Heartlands, baling a cart-full of dope in the Badlands, visited the Bermuda Triangle postdiluvian, the Andes Peruvian, the volcano Vesuvian; would inhale in the hail in the *der Vaterland,* would exhale to say "Wie Gehts!" in *die Mutterland,* and guest-singing "A Whiter Shade of Pale" with Procul Harum in a procured harem kept Him forgetfully hail-less hale and forever heart-full hearty. He played a Handel-piece beneath

the mantelpiece adorned and adored with shamrocks placed
out of place in the "out-of-plaice" sham rocks, the non-
traditional razz-a-ma-tazz made Him wonder, the traditional
jazz-a-ma-tazz made Him wander, He inadvertently tumbled
(once again !) into blunderbuss Gus when He stumbled
onto (another) wanderlust bus where He made such a fuss,
He gave a loud cuss as the rain in His ears caused his best
brains to rust, His man-wet trouser legs to lust for a woman's
sweat-moistened bust, His audition was commissioned for a
jug of ale and a crust, His clothes were all tattered, His head
never hattered, His shoes and socks on the cobblestones pat-
pitter, pit-pattered; His fish and chips always battered, His
uncle's matter-filled carbuncles never mattered, His oil wells
well wild-cattered, the Church of Day Saints most Lattered,
His conversations were all nattered and His thoughts were
all scattered by the robust winds of August, the augur gust
winds of Winter to be celebrated in Skits, played-out in Plays,
metered in Theatres, layered like linguini in cook-booking
lessons or sung like Puccini in book-cooking sessions, were
bent up and scent up to be born-alive beginning-down at the
fed-end but never torn down and sent down to die dead-end up
in a Dead End, to be wended and lended, mended and sended,
to be rendered and tendered by a physiatrist elemental, a
psychiatrist detrimental, saw the "second coming" in six days

59

with a Seventh Day Adventist, witnessed Monsieur Le Touth, a most famous fencist, have *les tooths* maxillary dentured and axillary indentured by Dr Paine, a new graduate dentist; watched Herr Abdo, a less infamous obeseist, have a colonic lavage and the liquid collage be inadvertently carved by Dr Payne, an old undergraduate Lentist; knew every holiday except on what Sunday Lent is, a nemesis with persist, filled fillings with his left wrist and would file filings with his right wrist, attacked decay with attrition, wrongs with admonition, advocated acts of contrition, and who always argued with incessant repetition that disintegrating dentition was a reversible condition that was undoubtedly and unmouthfully caused by extremely poor nutrition. *Ipso facto*.

Be Scene and Not Herd.

A tall-tale was bold-told in the uplands by a coven of hunch-backed, country-hearth bred, black-robed hags; a veritable malapertness of peddlers, who cultivated a murder of crows, wore bundles of rags, bred a rag of colts, rode a barren of mules, trained a stud of mares, used a drunkship of cobblers, sailed a drunk ship of fools, made a business of ferreting out a business of ferrets, sounded out a sounder of wild boar, rebounded out with a "bounder," a real bloody bore; got drunk with a glozing of taverners, fed a drift of swine (even snow drifts when adrift in snow-drifts), hunted nyes of pheasants but said "nays" to peasants, hunted a gang of elk, ate a clutch of eggs, used a sheath of arrows when hidden in the narrows, trapped a cete of badgers, clustered a muster of peacocks, laid seige to a sege of herons, herded a herd of curlews, praised the daily exaltation of larks, never obeyed the parliament of rooks and owls but took issue with what "parley meant" with crooks and towels, turned a field where runners been into a field for runner-beans, but the black-hatted *wica* with their wicker-mat sacks were shamelessly driven from Slovenia's lowlands by way of Armenia by a pontification of priests, a bench of bishops, a staff of servants with staves, a bunch of punch-drunken, cloven Brave-Heart, Scottish-bred Clue-less *Klutz* Clan with woven County overalls and proven City-oven white bread packed in much-proven, munch-proven, country-wide, whole-wheat, brown lunch-bags to a "brown-bag" lunch. Here they broke up the brunch, attendance was crunched, bathrooms were bunched, the coat-rooms were scrunched, the lunch-bunch were sucker-punched, the dunce-bunch were punch-drunk, the Dutch-bunch were tulip-bunched, the henchmen were hunched, there was a hunchback with a lunch-pack, a munch-Jack with a brunch-sack, never a dunce-lack but a punch-whack, a crunch-rack for a scrunch-knack, a *bungee* cord to take the slack, a "roadie" bunch of truckers Mack, a rowdy bunch of cluckers quack, a mountainside Yak, a biblical Zach, the brunch-bunch were baseball bunt, the hunch-bunch were basket-balled dunked, and the smallest Dallas Cowboy was hunted and punted, dented and insulted, his growth was so stunted as he was so forgetfully famished, forever infamous and foreverly famous as a footballing runt. *Very peditastellustic.*

On the Bloomsday Occasion....................... *(Play the First).*

On the Bloomsday Occasion of James Joyce (the Scholastic Irishman) meeting the 'Quare Fella on June 16th, 1904. Now just on a hunch *the Scholastic Irishman* was once reputed and twice disputed to have met the *Quare Fella* once one early evening in the lowlands at the dance Tarantella, and once one late morning in the uplands before the matinee Cinderella, and said "pleased to meet you, Oel Yelworc" to which the *Fella* and his accompanying *iijits* replied "and we are even *more* pleased to meet *you,* Semaj Ecyoj, and *Nollaig faoi shean is faoi mhaise duit* and *Blain Nua mhaith agat !*" And *"ein gutes, gesundes und gluckliches neues Jahr 2004"* replied the Joyce-voice "to you, to you too, and to you two, too" continued the voice-Joyce "and I am the death of endeavor and the birth of disgust" *ex cathedra, ex more, ex officio.* This life of great measure and the mirth of this gust concluded, though somewhat deluded, His early work only grist for the mill, filling the coffin of a document, the scabbard of a bill, the husk of a remittance, the bed-gown of a love letter, suitably placed for the shafts of malice, envy and detraction, the laws of the Universe annulled on behalf of a single petitioner confessedly unworthy, His frail ghost an outward and visible sign of an inward fear. "Now, now, James" comforts the fierce Ambrose Bierce (1842-1914) "you are an enlightened soul who prefers sweet wines to dry, sentiment to sense, humor to wit, and slang to clean Irish." "Maybe you should read to working-class audiences like me" says Charles Dickens of a Christmas Carol (25/12/1843 for British readers, 12/25/1843 for American readers) when he took Carol at Christmas to *A Christmas Carol* "as she lost nothing, misinterpreted nothing, followed everything closely, laughed and cried, and animated me to the extent that I felt as if we were both bodily going up into the clouds together." Recognizing the assembling swarm of additional *iijits* and low-heels, *craitheurs* and imbeciles, perambulators and automobiles, Joyce gasped "araagh, 'tis the *Quare Fella* himself, but you all have to be snappy to have a happy Miss taken or maybe unhappy to be sadly mistaken as I'm really Semaj Enitsugua Suisyola Ecyoj for long and that is the short of it, that is the fun of it and that is the furlong of it." "Well, *La Feile Padraig faoi mhaise agai !* anyway" replies the *Quare Fella* himself and the

63

queer fellers to themselves, "and I'm really Oel Leahcim
Yelworc for short but not for long and that is the throng of it."
Not taken aback or turning His back, but "sharp as a tack" as a
shark on attack, the J.A.A. Joyce in His G.A.A. voice to the
Quare Fella asks *"cur non mitto meos tibi, Oel Leahcim
Yelworc, libellos ? Ne mihi tu mittas, tuos ! Et versus scribere
posse te disertos affirmas, laberi quid ergo non vis ?"* "You got
it, Toyota," replies the bicycle-pedalling *Quare Fella.* "And one
more thing" says the tricycle-meddling *Scholastic Irishman,*
"you can tell Mr Bloom in the doom and the gloom of a rainy
afternoon in auld Ireland's doubting Dublin that his hundreth
Bloom's Day *Bloomsday* equerry and nice niece Annie's
anniversary from Galway's University is this year, being a two,
two noughts and a four, and there's a little something I want
you to do for me to celebrate the occasion." "And what is that,
Oh literary Christ?" asks the *Quare Fella.* "Write this down,
now, and get it translated from the *Ogham*, but be careful,
don't let happen to you'se like what happened to that yank
Joseph Smith feller in 1844 in New York, now y'hear." (*Ogham*
is an ancient Irish script of which the letters are represented by
groups of parallel lines that meet or cross at a straight base
line. It is believed to have originated in Ireland as a secret
script about around c.3 A.D.) Yet the *Scholastic Irishman* was
even more adamant than Adam Ant about getting it right. "No,

64

no, what you thought you heard was not what I said, what I said was not what I meant, what I meant to say you obviously didn't hear. So don't take or write it wrong even if I'm going to make a short story long. I didn't say what I thought, which is what I wanted you to hear, and as you only heard what I said, whatever I said I certainly didn't mean as you obviously didn't hear what I thought to say but only what you thought I meant, however meaningful you thought you heard me say it, as whatever was in my thoughts was what I wanted to say, and even if I didn't say it you know what I meant, no matter what I said, whatever I meant, whatever you heard, whatever you thought you heard, or whatever it was that I said." The *Quare Fella* acknowledged the un-knowing which cannot be known by knowingly acquiescing, "you didn't say anything that I heard, I didn't hear anything you said and that settles it" The ghostly Joyce-voice adjusted His sinews and adjunctively continued, before quietly getting in and jetting off on, petting on and jet-set offing in, going on and off, off and on, repeating *abra, abra, abra* before the barnacled Nora ever knew what *a bra* was, when the *Praecepta de Medicina* was written (second century), if Q. Severus Sammonicus was ever us, who *Ab, Ben* and *Ruach Acadosh* were, but that there was something very magical about *Abracadabra* every-time James Joyce (*l'agent provocateur*) would reach out and grab ya !" He was abstemious in pubs, abstentious from churches, arsenious to His enemies, caesious with Robert Wilhelm Bunsen, facetious with His friends and inexplicably fracedinous when trying to get His bowels in anatomical order and His vowels in alphabetical order. But the beta-blocker vegetarian, the soccer-playing Eskanderian, was holy alphabetic but never wholly diabetic, was holaphabetic but never peripatetic, would suddenly run on us and pun on us, pulled a spelling-gun on us, mulled a yelling bee on us, really pulled a fast-one on us, His onus His Opus, sent a pangram by telegram, a gangplank by Pan Am, an anagram by hologram, tipped Anglican clergy in a tippet, tipped Newcastle coal from a tipple, tippled with a tippy-toed tippler in a tavern, tip-toed up to a tipsy tipster in Malvern, led a tirade at a tip-top parade, tipped off the tip-off time at a basketball charade, and stereotyped a typical typographer to type "how piqued gymnasts can level six jumping razorback frogs" on us but just after He met us on to expose on and suppose on an alpha-betting abecedarian "A Bold Cavalier Did Everything For Greater Happiness In Jovial Kind, Letting Many New Officers Perform Quite Ridiculous Stunts To Utilize Very Worldly eXercises of Youthful Zen." It was flotsam and jetsam, Rodgers and Hammerstein, biceps and triceps, port and starboard, Bert and Ernie, trweeter and woofer, Gilbert and Sullivan, rack and ruin, Statler and

Waldorf, warp and weft, stalactite and stalagmite, Scylla and Charybdis, *x* & *y*, Siskel and Ebert, curds and whey, pitch and yaw, rack and pinion, Penn and Teller, and not a single detention but an honorable mention, to stand at attention without apprehension, to attend the ascension of St. Jeremy Jenson, no room for abstention, no tomb for descension, no groom for comprehension, no broom for retention, no doom for prevention, no gloom for convention, a bloom gentian for *presention*, a Bloom for dissention, a loom for extension, a boon for intention, a moon for dimension, high noon for contention, meet you soon at the convention, sing *loony tunes* without intervention, fling sea-flying loons with ostention, leave Harry Coombs without a pension, Harvard lampoon without tension, croon without pretension, and they lowered the boom with the utmost inattention, the gut-most incomprehension, the lamp post indention, the pot-roast distention, without any apprehension and left the Joyce-Voice in an orderly State (without-a-mention), impaled on a stanchion of a bridge most suspension in a most disorderly state of complete hypertension. Respectfully with condescension and reflectively without prehension, the Great Man *Himself* with great circumvention then muttered "I am *fe mhoid bheith saor,* and I'm writing to you *thar toinn do rainig chugainn,* and speaking on behalf of Myself and My family, Ireland for me is *sean tir ar sinsir feasta."*

And with the young May moon beaming bright, the ecclesiastic, enthusiastic, fantastic, gymnastic and *Scholastic Irishman* pedaled madly through the old day's night, gladly into the new day soon becoming bright, sadly down over the hill and towards the light, badly spinning farther away forwards and grinning further away backwards, and mellow-yellow yelling with expectorant spelling "and may you live as long as you want and never want as long as you live, dance as if no one was watching, sing as if no one was listening, dream like you were going to live forever, and live as though you would die today." And with that, the break-away voice, the break-of-day Joyce, the male-faced strider in a condescending voice, muttered kindly after the pale-faced horse-less rider clattering blindly alongside the mail-paced rider-less horse nattering kindly, "and may the best day of your past be the worst day of your future." *Was ein Mann*, whatta Man, Amen and *Amein.* And with that He was gone, the Cosmos devoid, an un-interrupted stream of sub-conscious literary prose, an un-interrupted dream of unconscious poetic literature, from the alphabet Devanagari to Du Maurier's Svengali, sitting between a Diva and a Dewan on a divan, a dialogue dyslectic with diaphoretic selective, a passionate diapason, a Sonata *passionata,* no Elliott wasteland but a Helliot waist-band for *this* Voice, *this* Joyce, who never measured His life in coffee cups and tupperware, but pleasured His wife with toffee-ups and underwear ! *Mens sana in corpore sano !*

Autopsy of Synopsy of Play the First.

Of the three fellers twice, the tree-feller Joyce has His *bon-*satirized, non-plagiarized plays played all around to Irish minors, IRA Majors, English miners and PTA whiners in the Theatre-in-the-Round (even when full with literary sound), played to "squares" in the theatre-in-the-square (even when empty and nobody there), and conceded to hold concert with non-disputedly disrespectable, non-delectably disreputable, Lynard Skynard; had dessert with reputedly most respectable, delectable and reputable, Medical Assistant Abigail "Abbie;" the Scottish-born cabby was crab-apple crabby; the skinned-lizard appetizers, the scissored salad, the buzzard-gizzard soup in the three-tiered dinner served by a eye-visored Wizard to skinny lounge-lizard Lynard wasn't too shabby; the acting in the meager theatre Abbey delighted "eager-beaver" Hayes Gabby, although the dialogue was diabolically blabby and was constantly interrupted by a very noisy "babby." The ushers were gabby, the player's costumes very price-conscious savvy, at the sad parts the audience became with their handkerchiefs very "dabby," the dancers were flabby, their backs very quite scabby, and in the after-hours "honky tonks" there were "wonky donk" Monks decidedly grabby, feeling up altar-boys on the marble-slabs slabby, and all that was needed to stop it was a couple of Sir John's "Peelers" or a really good Rabbi. When cold-old Joyce ascetic, his *corpus delictic*, heard this bold-told "bubble-and-squeak" frenetic His tone-told, bone-bold, cone-told, phone-fold, hone-hold, Joan-gold, love rolled, moan-hold, roan-sold, zone-wold, voice-specific condemned dyslectic literature-unsure speak from the wayward and highways, day wards and byways, cowards and low-ways, live and let die-ways, hillsides and wave-ways, mountainsides and paved-ways, fountain-sides and pay-days, and sat in the out-of-State diner for a very late dinner. Whiner the winner, the kinder the thinner, the finder the kinner, the grinder the Lynard, the minder the Skynard, the winder the sinner, the binder the tinner, from the winter Hollywood Heights to the summer sailing doldrums, in a manner most beholding, gave a tenner with a scolding, "flipped the bird" with a cuckolding, paid cash for a withholding, watched the Silversmiths selling wrist-watches with gold rings, matched the Goldsmiths selling finger-matches with silver-rolled dings, observed the fraught teachers taming their study-less, clue-less, young-student bold things; from realtors with their holdings to merchants with their sold things, treated his hot flashes with flush coldings in the launderies with their foldings, from the DYI's in UK with their mouldings to Lowe's and Home Depot in USA with their moldings, from the young ones getting older to the elders getting olding, told tales and sold sales in retirement homes to the *nouveau* families with new cars with their new "dings," trucked bales over dales to new homes with wet-bars and new swings, survived old Wales and fierce gales in *faux* homes for "Jack-Tars" with buffalo-wings, selected males and rejected females for Baseball's Hall-of-Fame excluding the *le barre* for small-breasted swings, selected females and rejected males for "Take All" balls-of-flame including *Le Bare* for large-breasted things, but was exquisitely gentle when visiting the gentile and very charming, downwardly mobile and upwardly noble, decidedly geriatric "sweet, little, old things" in their gerontocomium condominiums. *In loco parentis.*

A Night on the Town.

The Dubliners in the London nights, the Publicans under the Dublin lights, the Nubians under the Pyramid lights all watched "on call" as the drug traffic stalled at the shady, dull Stop lights, Naval-full patrons enthralled at the lady-full "Red lights," the "Big Apple" visitors confused by the navel-full Orange lights, the dancing Poles giving the "Go-Go" dancing, pole-dancers the legs-up, leggy-full Green light, mayhem in Mayfair, madness at the May Fair, Harley Street with bone surgeons, Marley Silas with

71

bony sturgeons, Barley silos with bonny curmudgeons, let's all get a valet, eat at the buffet and go to the ballet. It's an enchanting experience with *enchainement*, you can chat afterwards at the *entrechat*, the connoisseurs delight at the camber of the *cambre*, the patrons all know what the *changement*, they eat sauerkraut at the *saut*, sip jelly at the *jete*, taste *fois gras* at the *fouette,* it's "Ce n'est pas" at the *pas*, the *pas de deux*, the *pas de quatre*, they pout at the *pirouette*, are relieved to relive the *releve*, with an *encore* of the enigmatic *variation* (music by Elgar) where the *plies* are like pliers, the *sur les points* are sur le pont, it's all you can do to do the Can-Can *terre a terre* with your feet on the ground. The audience goes mad, the dancers are glad, the visitors are sad but leave glee-ing and tea-ing (with cream and sugar, please) at the tourist sites, the tourists weeping and tearing on seeing the "welcome visitor" sights, their rainy shoes getting grubby, their grainy clothes very scrubby, each loving wife with her hubby downing drinks in the Pubby, the rainy-grainy lovers feeling each other up and down in the cubby, the Brooklyn Dodgers left for the West Coast, the Bronx dogs stayed on the East Coast, the "cool cats" hot-dogging it in the bushes very shrubby, the tin-working Tinkers rubbing elbows very "rubby," Jason and the "fatties" becoming Way "Subbie," the Argonauts "aw, go on now," and that left only the "thinners" to eat up their dinners, become gourmet sinners and get really deleterious and serious about getting beer-belly "tubby."

Qoud sicca redolet palus lacuna, piscinae vetus aura quod marinae,

quod pressa piger hircus in capella, lassi vardaicus quod evocati,

maestorum quod anhelitus reorum, quod spurcae moriens lucerna

veritae, quod vulpis fuga, viperae cubile, mallem quam quod oles

olere.

Mid-Life Re-Booting.

From the ghettos with their grime, crime and slime; the barrios

with their shooting, polluting and executing; to the suburbs

with their flash, trash and cash; their generic computers

booting, their cables comminuting, their owners commuting,

their programs computing, Confucius confuting, the politicians

"darn tooting," the lawyers constituting, the sheriffs' deputing,

the criminals disputing, the Irish whisky diluting, the orchestral

flautists fluting, the fruit-flies on the flautist's flutes fruiting,

the flies fruiting and flauting on the flying fruits flutes, the fries

in France french-frying, the motel models high-falooting, the

Dallas Cowboys galooting, the BMW's horn tooting, the non-

jailing judges imputing, the prize prison wardens instituting,

the snobby robbers looting, the robbing snobbers mooting, the

sober sobbers trans-muting, the idealist ideas off-shooting,

the corralling gunslingers each other precisely out-shooting, the

free-booting rapids the choral kayakers over-shooting, the

class changes and grass ranges the computers permuting,

the land-lady liars the dissenting renters persecuting, the grimy rust and slimy dust industries of the rich Industrialists polluting, the thorny attorneys the hapless victims prosecuting, the hat-less "oldest profession" ladies with the most-fat "newest concessions" self-prostituting, the newest confession Boy Scouts two-finger saluting, the inner cities ghettos reconstructing and their barrio Charters reconstituting, the Dick Armey Army recruiting, the dick-happy Navy re-suiting, the ancient Marine Corps *Semper Fidelis,* the impatient Air Force *Adeste Fidelis,* the beer-swilling cheerleaders up-rooting, the near-willing Mexicans roofing, the seer-milling middle-schoolers scooting, the athletic coaches substituting, the pathetic roaches de-instituting, the tailors up-suiting, the train whistles tooting, the jeans on the genes of the chromosomes transmuting, the footballers booting, the storm-winds up-rooting, the sty-fed sows carry on rooting, the wry lead ring-roads re-routing, there was no Peyton Place anywhere for literature-unsure speak in the marvel and mystery of *His* literature-sure geek world. *Et nunc et semper.*

His Not-So-Great Depression.

Oh ! Listen ! My only tried and true literal brothers and literary sisters to the lisping and limping, lying and libeling, limiting and lingering, littering and livening words of your

74

humble narrator ! The non-Nobel noble *Scholastic Irishman* became apoplectic, was not fit to chide, wanted to lay down and die, no more time would He bide, was fit to be tied, then had a fit and *was* tied, became desuetude from the Quaaludes, desultory from the basement, used words category when He didn't know what the base meant, used words derogatory when to Purgatory was sent, played the guitar in the bar though sick with catarrh, appointed thirteen unlucky sallow fellows who all played the cello, even paid twelve "even-Steven" trumpeters to whistle *clair de lune* in the daylight most mellow, left eleven *gigolos* with piccolos un-sate at the phony Symphony gate-post yellow, picked ten apples in pairs in the Gulag most Archipelago, trumpeted nine peers at "toothpick" Nick's nickel-and-dime stores you must bellow, ate eight pears in pairs with a leftover apple and jello, was in "Seventh Heaven" with French horns and Sony saxophones, say "hello", (on *Saturday Night Live !* Tracy Morgan says "hello, I'm Brian Fellow"), placed six bare bears in the pit, five loud lions in the loge, four brain-less malcontents with arm-full falconry in the arm-less armchair balcony, three blind bats in a cave, even had time to admire the lovely, lean, lithe and lissome hind-legs on a "babe," wrote rave short stories about his brave feats in the not-long-enough seats for his very long feets, became desultory from the

second storey with impermanent glory, cited oratory from
a first story by a permanent Tory, put Tommy Dorsey in the
Orchestra pit with a helmet-full pith, fast snow-ploughed the
slow crowd, enlightened the high-brows, chopped off the low
boughs, herded the Hereford cows, Suez-steered the Arab
Dhows, met the elite "here-and-now's," avoided domestic
rows, corralled the wild sows, remade broken wedding vows,
acknowledged audience "wows" and came out blowing
odors of odes between the droves in the groves, the pleats
in the seats, the scarce rows of not-very-scary scare-crows,
the scary scarce crows sitting in the stands, the many wary
scary crows shitting on the lands, 'twas a sign of the times,
a space between the lines, a car-full of fines, a tree-full of
vines, a stage-full of mimes, a wood-full of pines, a cellar-full
of wines, a hillside of mines, a book-full of rhymes, a dollar-
full of dimes, all dole-full and soul-full, woe-full and doe-
full, praying and decaying, He set friend against foe, Freud
against Defoe, got mis-fits Curly, Larry and Moe to match
wits with schizophrenics Allan and Edgar Poe, compared
Irish Yeats against England's Keats, introduced Oliver Twist
to Oliver Goldsmith, ended up at Crystal Palace in a chrysalis
of degeneration, was sent down to Crewe Station for his
charybdis of denigration, got crippled in Staffordshire by
Sir Stafford Cripps for his scylla of hagiography and would

not never-ever in any kind of weather tolerate any nay-say derogatory about dear Lady Gregory. Good manners never go out of style. *A Posteriori.*

The Palindromic Dubliner.

Once in Austria asked Franz Haydn "in France is the hay done ?" Twice in France saw Bonaparte but ever-only once with his bones apart, and for inexplicable tripe and fully explainable thrice, the anagrammatical Sotades of Maronea insulted Ptolemy II and was encased in lead and drowned. A pal in Rome wrote a Palindrome *Anne, I vote more cars race Rome to Vienna*, whereas W. H. Auden, alone in his garden decided that *Sums are not set as a test on Erasmus* and *Norma is as selfless as I am, Ron.* Ferdinand de Leseppes had a plan for a plane o'er a plain, *A man, a plan, a canal : Panama* yet was ever Bonaparte *able was I ere I saw Elba,* so hence-fourth Elba was Joyce ere Ecyoj saw Abel, Abel was Cain ere Niac saw Lebanon, Lebanon was Nora ere Aron saw Nonabel, Nonabel was Tinkerbell ere Llebreknit saw Melba, Ablem was Aaron ere Nora Barnacle saw W. H. Auden who wrote that *"Isobel, with her leaping breast, pursued me through a summer."* Rather Dan Rather rather than Dan Lebosi, with his gaping vest, pursue Cocaine 'Lil or Morphine Sue through a bummer. While sailing the Bodensee He always did ever see the van

77

that Vanderbilt built that was banned on the Autobahn, was butter-thumb, numb-struck with dumb luck on His van Gogh yacht; brought up the vanguard to check on the Czech vanguard who was checking the route that His *mach-3* van Gogh van would go; would butter-finger, malinger, harbinger on His non-stop, stop-watch clock and then dance the tango; put on His Van Allen radiation belt, supported President Van Buren, connected His Van de Graaff generator, took "man-the-walls" courses to defeat van der Waals's forces, didn't let the demons land in Van Diemen's Land, critiqued and edited Mark and Carl Van Doren, *did* let Sir Anthony Van Dyck with a Lady, but found most crying Dutchmen and the host Flying Dutchman with their razors cocked and just too weird with a Vandyke beard, couldn't holler in a Vandyke collar, crowned His hair in Vandyke brown, got high-brow with His eye-brows and in Vlaardingen everyone listened to Schubert, sipped on their sherbets, asked "is that you, Bert ?" turned on their house-alerts, and never forgot to ever-say "Hi ! Hubert" to Huybrecht van Eyck. *Gesundheit !*

Pub-Grub Down at the Old Bull-and-Bush.

In London's East End within earshot of the bells of St Mary-le-Bow in Cheapside He couldn't *Adam and Eve* the palaver, lived apart from the *Artful Dodger*, paid His *Duke of Kent*, would *Ball and Chalk* up the *Apples and Pears*, a quick *Jimmy Riddle*, a *Bob Hope* in the *Boat Race*, a quick *Gregory Peck* at *Barnet Fair*, select *Whistle and Flute* and match *Peckham Rye*, a new *Dicky Dirt* is not going to hurt, style a neat *Tit for Tat* on His *Loaf of Bread*, hitch *Ascot Races* in places, would *Dog and Bone* a *Battlecruiser*, joy-ride in a *Jam Jar*, the *Frog and Toad* was *Mork and Mindy* but the *Currant Bun* was out, the *Rub-a-Dub* served *Aristotle*, drank His first *Cock and Hen*, was down to His last *Lady Godiva*, an empty *Sky Rocket* without *Bread and Honey*, got *Brahms and Liszt*, would *Kick and Prance* to the *Aunt Joanna*, stuck an *Oily Rag* in His *North and South*, told *Porky Pies*, went berserk for *Bristol City*, found one with *Syrup of Figs*, *Tom-foolery* and nice *Alan Wickers*; His *China Plate* gave Him *Chalk Farm*, and when *Boracic Lint* found the publican's *Bricks and Mortar*, she was *Skin and Blister* to His Trouble and Strife, *Sweeney Todd* was called, they wanted *Brass Tacks*, it was *Darby and Joan*, *Barnaby Rudge* gave Him the *Butcher's Hook*, he didn't say *Dicky Bird*, there was no time to *Mickey Bliss*, His *Mince Pies* were bloodshot, when His *Daisy Roots* removed the *Pen and Ink* of the *Plates of Meat* was *Richard the 3rd*, He felt *Hampton Wick*, He looked like *Brown Bread*, was radically *Hank Marvin*, the *Dustbin Lids* were rummaged and scrummaged for *Tea Leaves*, He was ready for a *Pony and Trap*, His *Khyber Pass* was bagged,

79

Cobbler's Awls were ragged, *Chalfont St Giles* were snagged, the *Peeler* was *Mutt and Jeff*, the *Rosser Jam Jar* was artfully dodging the *Lionel Blairs*, and all He wanted forever was a really hot cuppa *Rosie Lee*. In London's West End within slingshot of the belles of St Graham Le Saux in Dearside, He couldn't *blag* the *Polari*, it was *dolly cackle* to *charper* a *dona*, to *vada* a *palone*, but the *bona omi* and *mince omi-palone's* were so *dolly*, they all had the *clobber*, the *dinarly*, such *fantabulosa drag*, their *shush bag* a *slap*, *vogue*, and when they left the *lattie* for a *buvare* just everyone, dahling, would *vada* their *trolling* whether *Todd Sloane* or not, *ogle* their *mince*, *bugle* their *dish*, *finagle* their *lallies*, *eagle* their *eek*, *beagle* their *riah*, *regal* their *yews*, not one *nanty naff*, always a *bona nochi* for a *bijou mangarie*, and when *narker lilly* approached, would talk *fantabulosa balonie* before he would *scarper and flow* in the Scarpa Flow. *Casus belli.*

American Gastronomy (or Eating with the Yanks).

In the United States the Voice-restaurant was Nefretiti, the Joyce-art was graffiti, but the Joyce-appetite was easily stated when in the diner stated that for breakfast He wanted the *crowd*, *Adam and Eve*, them to *wreck 'em* on the *crowded Adam 'n' Eve*, over the *bridge* and *clean up the kitchen*, *warts* and *axle grease on a raft*, don't spare the *sea dust*, *yum-yum* and tomato *hemorrhage, in the alley* with a *squeeze, burn the British, zeppelins in a fog,* followed by *shingles with a shimmy* (made especially for Jimmy), bring a *java* for Joe with *moo juice* and without *sand,* also some *belch water* and a *bucket of hail;* some *joe* for Ava, *no cow,* with sand (so *pass the gravel train*), and a *life-preserver.* Before lunch would hound the hounds on the island, for lunch ordered *hounds on an island* (extra *breath*), would try *two cows* but *make them cry,* or perhaps tell them to *put out the lights and cry,* some pepper for Mike and some salt for Ike, and never appreciated the *looseners* giving Him a good run for His money. For dinner in the diner with Dinah ordered a *splash of red,* Murphy (in his jacket) ordered *murphy's* in *their* jackets with non-morning, non-mourning *wreaths,* light with the *side-arms, Adam's ale* (hold the *hail*), and always took dessert *on wheels,* loved *Eve with a lid on,* a *bucket of cold mud* and always went light with the *lumber* before a deep slumber. *Guten nacht.*

Grecian Attitudes.

In Greece was amused by Nine Muses without fuses, the pyrogenic progeny of mighty Zeus and flighty Mnemosyne, and appeared in Pieria at the head of the Universe and the foot of Mount Olympus. Three *mouseions* each for Plato's plates, Aristotle's bottles and Ptolemy's One chamber pot.

Clio loved his story, history *lontano*; Melpomene tragically loved tragedy *patetico*, Thalia laughed *alla Italia* at comedic comedy most *fugato*, Urania gazed at the astronomic stars *grave*, Euterpe usurped flauting flutes *forte-piano*, Tersichore played harpsicorde *risvegliato*, mine own Polyhymnia mimed alone *slargando*, Erato never erred with her love poetry *scherzando*, and Calliope eloped with her epochally epic poetry in motion most *lusingando*. The haughty Megaera was jealous, the naughty Tisphone was the blood avenger, the sought-after Alecto was unceasing, three daughters of gay Gaia, all created from the blood of Uranus (the un-godly Melaena) after a catastrophic castration by Cronus (auwe !) witch got the eeky-geeky, sneaky-peaky, beaky-weaky, freaky-leaky, meaky-peeky, sqeaky-queeky, reeky-tiki, greasy-Greeky Gods furious, the "in-your-face" Erinyes were "in-your-place" Erin knees and were more kindly thought of as Eumenides. He met Hermaphroditus who wouldn't indite us, Hermes Trismegistus who 'dissed us, saw Hermione all alone, handsome Hercules had herpes and had to limp-along in the hepathalon, Goddess Hera was never there, Heraclitus had haemorrhoids, Heraclius was comatose, Herodotus never wrote us, Hippocrates had arthritic knees, Hippomenes was riding sleds, found out that Helen of Troy was a boy, was unable to mount Helena, raised hell with Helios, and after a summer term with heartworm, returned heart-broken to Hoboken with His very last token. *Quod erat demonstrandum.*

Roman Platitudes.

In Italy He hated the Paparazzi, loved the Mamarazzi, adopted the bambinarazzis, met the non-medical Medici's, avoided the medical deadici's, said "bon giorno" to the *literati* and "arrivederci" to the *illiterati,* never an obscene gutterance, always a precious utterance, and by word and by deed, by sword and by seed, in *Romans 11:33-36* "from Jer-USA-lem and as far around as Il-lyr'i-*cum*," got wolf twins Romulus and Remus, who though somniferous would redeem us, got Jupiter Pluvius to blaspheme us in front of the populace and Nicodemus, his chaste wife beauteous who would delightfully scream at us, his legions most duteous looked exceptionally mean at us, the Emperor Augustus would desultory gleam at us, Anthemius would dream about us, Magnentius would out-scheme us, Petronius would out-clean us, Galerius would lean on us, Maximus would out-team us, Scottie would up-beam us, the barley would out-ream us, the strawberries would cream us, and with Pliny-full insight and plentiful outside the volcano Vesuvius exploded unseen on us. On the east bank of the Tiber inside the Aurelian Wall the Roman Emperors rode horses on the Esquiline, Procopius found out that sorghum

gave him a sore gum on the Palatine, Aemilian ascended
Aventine in Advent, Caligula made Capitoline their capital,
Quintillus drank quinine on top of Quirinal, Valentinian
chased four-legged vermin up Viminal, Gallienus held picnics
with Emperor Caesar Titus Aelius Hadrianus Antoninus
Augustus Pius (a.k.a. Antoninus Pius) on the sides of the
Caelian, they then took off their shades, silenced their lathes,
chained up their slaves, manned the stone barricades, invited
the Quaids, any fighting their elders would swiftly dissuade,
any frightening their enemies would quietly evade, gave all
their young school-children their summertime grades, closed
their eyes while the young virgins bathe, the young girls in
turn with their hair they would braid, embowering their heads
with flowers in a perfumed brocade, their immodest bodices
glimmering with shimmering jade, 'twas a mad masquerade,
the young Senators they successfully and seductively
persuade, the old tenors tentatively and sentimentally
serenade, young-male affections for young female confections
were part of the trade, the sentries watched closely while
the young Caesars wade, then made amorous love with
their clamorous maids (remember what that was like before
there was no scourge of Aids), they were safe from the
Neopolitans and their most frequent raids, they pre-empted
the Milanos with their silent ambuscades, ran the wrath of

the Risorgimentos and their united blockades, no cannon-
fodder for the Vatican and its catechism cannonade, and
while the setting sun fades through the climbing pines glade,
they all fell asleep in the petting-zoo shade. And beneath the
dove-shaping awnings that the clinging vines made, 'twixt
the love-making dawnings that the singing pines bade, each
laid in the position that sixty-nine made, each one en*cum*ber
in an all-over slumber, restful and love-full, bosom-full and
Eros-full, affection-full and devotion-full, emotion-full and
passion-full, affection-full and ardor-full, pulchritudinous and
beauteous, libidinous and smitten, their post-whoring snoring,
rhythmically and sporadically, creeping inaudible through the
vines in the vales and the vineyards in the valleys; the music of
the Gods made audible in the warbling birdsongs, the snorting
of the hogs creating poems out of the bubbling brook sounds,
the soft breezes bequeathing the flowering scents of the
towering vents, silently crying and sighing, the warm afternoon
on it's own bosom dying, a flower-lei garland all-over the far
land, all peaceful and bliss-full, all geese-full and kiss-full,
chaste limbs and sated lambs, fountains and weir-dams; the
winds of Heaven flowing serene, the waters of Earth bubbling
careen, the veils of the evening dropping shimmering-sheen,
wax-purple and wheat-grass green, through the whispering
and singing, whistling and dreaming, warbling and sleeping,

Seven Hills of Rome. *Nimiast miseria nimis pulchrum esse hominem.*

Irish Literary Latitudes.

From the Italian wolf-born Romulus and Remus with their most rebuttal avenge, to the Irish Wolfe Tone's "Populous and Seamus" with their most subtle revenge, they turned the language of their oppressors from English tea-cup and saucery into the linguistics of their confessors as Irish re-coup and sorcery, and from jittery "Black and Tan" dwarfs made literary "*Craic* and Flan" noble Nobel giants out of Yeats, Shaw, Beckett and Heaney. From Tipperary butter to Copenhagen stutter, the World is far better for O'Casey and Kavanagh, O'Brien knew the "Old-Grey-Fellow," and would you ever believe it, Behan once on a Brendan voyage twice spotted the *Quare Fella.* Once a Goldsmith, a smooth-tongued writer eating dessert in *The Deserted Village* told a Silversmith, a crude-tongued blighter beating dirt in *The Pillaged Desert* that he preferred to let Dickens write about Oliver Goldsmith, let Bill Sykes ask Oliver Twist "what the Dickens was going on," let Fagin get the Artful Dodger to "dodge" furtive Nancy, let the Artful Dodger get Fagin to "Pagan" a lodger, *then* get Nancy to "fancy" Sir Roger "the codger," let General Motors' Dodge Division get upset with Ford Motor Company for letting Mr. and Mrs. Dodge drive a Ford because they couldn't afford a Dodge, let Ford Motor Company get upset with General Motors's Dodge Division for letting Mr. and Mrs. Ford drive a Dodge because they wanted to "dodge" a Ford. All this was enough leave to leave Joyce wool-knitting very neat, word-splitting very complete, tobacco-spitting in the street, under-arm sweating in the peat, hot pissing in the sleet, romantic wishing in the heat, tongue-kissing in the wheat, new-born sucking at the teat, barley-cutting in the wheat, quietly sitting on the toilet seat, noisily shitting in the toilet peat, there was nowhere to meet in order to right the wrong or wring the wrong out of the write that you're reading. *Pessime !*

The Linguist as Ventriloquist.

Up to now His out-penned gun was blunted, His out-gunned pen was stunted, He would defend right up to the end His right plays and playwright, autobiography and stenography, historical novels and hysterical quarrels, The Biography Channel and Coco Chanel, and even the biography of Coco Chanel on Coco Chanel's channel. He spoke Chinese to Subrahmanyan Chandrasekhar in Chandernagore, solicited Changchiakou in Chinese Changchun, spoke Indian to comedic chameleons in Ceylon, if looks could kill His books would thrill with un-extinguished morals and extinguishable brightly-colored corals,

87

they would out-sell and out-yell with non-extinguishable flames and insolvable games, to take their place on the shelf with the 1st Act of Richard II, the 2nd Act of Richard III, the 3rd Act of Henry V, the 4th Act of Henry VIII, the 1st Part (4th Act) of Henry IV, the 2nd Part (5th Act) of Henry V and He personally vowed to make that *His* last act of a dying man if *He* ever got to live that long, and that was the short of it. So to Jimmy-Jimmie James Joyce, the Atoll Bimini voice, the literary *vox populi*, goes a most honorable mention, defies all convention, a honorarium invention, honor guard at attention, honorific detention, *honoris causa* retention, honorary society dissention, honor system intention, honoree with affection, honors of war insurrection, horrific dissection, Honshu direction, Honolulu connection, and for a time aurific and grandific, beatific and classific, colorific and deific, humorific and magnific, omnific and pacific, pontific and prolific, pulsific and scientific, terrific and vivific, and to anyone all bored it's everyone "all aboard" for the *honorificabilitudinitatibus* of this loving and laboring Love's Labors Lost. *Ne plus ultra.*

The Ventriloquist as Linguist.

Bad enough that Sir Brendan O'Behan accepted *"The Quare Fellow"* and denied Socrates yet denied Hippocrates but accepted hypotheses that short guys wore long johns, long

John's told short lies, long-gone's tore short-ties, doggone's deplore goodbye's, short guys were long-gone's with long-moans that made whores wearing short-one's, long guys were *bon hommes* with short bones that raid stores baking hot buns, came un-glued and argued that boxers wore jockey shorts and jockeys wore boxer shorts, and always had "A hungry feeling come o'er me stealing, And the mice were squealing in my prison cell, And that old triangle went jingle jangle, Along the banks of the Royal Canal" yet criticized critics who wrote *critiques* on *"Mating for God, Oh !"* (which made *sui generis* Beckett crawl back behind the blackthorn), *"Trapp's First Gate"* (which Hazel Beckett wood deck it with witch hazel *hamamelidaceae*), *"A Spoon For The All Forgotten"* (glitch-made O'Neill kneel), *"The Best Play, Bhoy, is 'Wayne's World'"* (Whipsnade John Millington Synge cringe at the Zoo), *"The Tincture of Victorian Pray"* (which bade the sane Wilde insane), *"The Salad of Reading Gaol while reading 'Goal ?"* (witch-doctor the insane Oscar sane), *"If you never go to Pubs in Town,"* (switch-blade Kavanagh Patricidal), *"The Medicinal Cabinet Recitative"* (witch-maid Yeats Butler supercilious Well-I-am), *"The Golden Stile"* (witchcraft William Yeats super-bilious ill-I-am), *"Limitation of Maurice"* (which paid Jonathan Swift very slowly), *"Post Haste, Prattle of the Cooks"* (which trade slow Jonathan very swiftly), *"Realization"* (which engaged Goldsmith's wit at the witenagemot), *"John's Bull tethered by Land"* (Shaw weathered by Great Britain's other shore) and that the old repertories *"The Cow and The Szars"* and *"June and the Peacock"* made O'Casey's "you-know-where" pain return twice again, and from a mystique acclamatory, a boutique exclamatory, an antique excitatory, an oblique promontory to a negligent antiquity, an irreverent iniquity, a malevolent obliquity, a penitent ubiquity which was supposedly Celt, purportedly felt, supportively knelt and ultimately helped by purposely-kelped, don't leave a welt, hit below the belt, by a hand dealt, let out a yelp and insert yer suppositories, which immediately made O'Casey once again OK, see ....

Wild Oscar Wilde.

Wilde made his mark on society but not very quietly, made a lark of sobriety but very insightfully, disrespected the Deity very impolite-fully, admonished the Laity for their secret impropriety, astonished public editors with his astounding mediety, respected young children for their awestruck, sweet piety; loved ladies' noses for their beautiful variety, would astonish the gloved ladies with his indolent notoriety, would detest the foul-smelling drunkards for their constant insobriety, would admonish the critics for their in-constant contrariety, detested cowards and "craw-thumpers" for their ridiculous impiety, would always thank school-teachers for their educated omniety, would castigate unscrupulous politicians over their pot-bellied satiety, always repulsed the dirge-full clergy for their alter-wine inebriety, loved the Catholic Nun teachers for their ebullient ebriety, shoved the non-Catholic preachers into non-ubiquitous ubiety, would rebuke his many readers for their expansive anxiety, ridiculed his doubters for their insidious dubiety, disenfranchised the vain Vatican Vicars for their opulent *luxuriety,* preferred a torn marquee in a field, fought an old marquise on appeal, sued the Moscow "red" factions for dismantling a John Phillips Marquand book before it was read, said the right things about the writings but the wrong things about Donald Robert Perry Marquis, book-marked his many letters of marque, was night-parked by a *savant* servant in Marrakech, was nerved by a Marquesan in a turban on a tour-bus in Morrocco, had a Polish polisher polish his marquetry floor, had a foolish abolisher re-polish his Polish nail-polish more, relished his horse-radish relish under a marquisette awning, the yawning Marquess of Queensberry ruled "you can't hide" to a fawning wild Oscar, thus warning Wilde Oscar gone wild to stop drooling at Coole, stop "breaking the rules" and "let this *thing* die," but Lady Windemere's most loyal fan just couldn't live without the young marquis of Kingsplum asleep at his side, and being in yearnest, and absolutely his durnest, with his Oxford-book learnest, and with his sexuality turnest, it was out of the fire and into the furnace, and in all-consummate Earnest, that was The *very* Importance of Being Oscar. *A priori.*

Waiting for Beckett.

In the "john" John Millington Synge after a binge always piddled *On the Fringe,* trimmed his moustache with a singe, rimmed his mousetrap with a hinge, colored his hair with a tinge which made "cuddly" Dudley Moore cringe, bubbly Demi Moore winge, so no more of Dudley Moore with his HMS and even less of Demi Moore with her PMS. All-observant Joyce would start drinking less reclusively in the pub yet never prevented "rocking" Robin Cook from performing the outrageous, would always upstage us, and polished his art with a good resonating fart, deliciously tart, and forever was shrinking, never publicly thinking, yet winking and stinking as He practised his art. Cuddly Dudley was always Moore, famously infamous to the core, and "Rocking Robin" Cook was always less, infamously famous with that look, and while you whistle-while-you-shirk, thistle-in-the-dirt, gristle in the work, William Butler started getting "older and grayer, and even more tired and full of sleep" until in a pre-prandial

state on a post-sundial date he could never figure out where
Maud Gonne was gone. Any snob-type or *gobshite* from the
Connemara *Gaeltacht* can beat the "bum's rush" at Yankee
Stadium or turn a Church-on-the-hill conundrum into a
Batman riddle, hidden inside an Agatha Christie mystery
and secreted into an Edward Elgar enigma variation, easily
wrapping sublime inside a warm overcoat, puffing perfumed
presence through a literary cigar, distilling cultivated charm
into a post-prandial brandy, and delightfully observing
such *Anam Cara* wisdom being force-fed to the starving
and thirsting, carving and bursting, illegitimate and literate,
legitimate and illiterate, *sans Catholic* Darth Vader crusaders
and *sins Demonic* barf-raider invaders. Have a shot of glue and
stick around. Joyce then raced Swift against Jonathan, became
irrational with teacher Miss Anna in the National *Scoil Eanna,*
made John Milling's son cringe and John Millington Synge
twinge when "hey, hey, J.J." was once asked on a pay-day
by newly bankrupt Tennyson "can I please have a penny, son ?"
to which *He* replied "I really don't have that many, mon,"
and even *then* played croquet on the tennis lawn with Lord
Tennyson's lawn-tennis son, did not know where that portly
bel canto Portobello fellow Patrick Kavanagh was from and
was told "I'm *not* from Cavan, naw, I'm from Monaghan, now !"
Spell me backwards, spell me forwards, I'm always the same,

I'm a town in auld Ireland, can you tell me my name ? And who wrote a newspaper column about the IRA columns who went solemnly marching past Padraic Colum's column most solemn ? Take an egg and beat it ! Coy Joyce in Belfast would always butt-out on sad days and went Oxford Wilde when Irish Oscar got his American Oscar, but in Paris ole Samuel Beckett would always butt-in on "Happy Days" and went "laughing wild amidst severest woe." *Eadem, sed aliter.*

Cricket on a Sticky Wicket.

Out-of-luck Joyce once lost His golf ball in a thicket, and perchance, by chance, met irreparably disreputable "Chance the gardener," the soon to be indisputedly reputable Chancely Gardiner, then went out and bought a season-full ticket for the county-match cricket, and in the garden by chance met no better ticket-seller than yes debtor, steeple-peeper, no-battery beeper, ole Auntie-hero Peter Sellers, his Dream Team a bounty-team in the County-team cricket, falling from the table-topping pillars to the table-bottom cellars, so he took "just the ticket" and through the turnstile would click it, quite unlike Tony Lock, Peter Stock and three Woking carols; quirky-bite Vinnie Jones in Lock, Stock and Two Smoking Barrels where our anti-hero "was eighteen, and I've got a bullet; I've got my finger on the trigger, and I'm going to pull it." 'Twas a *scene* to be *seen* when out-of-the-muck, full-of-pluck Joyce watched Samuel "who ran well" Beckett, that ole "stick in the mud" get stuck in the muck on a muddy and mucky, very "sticky wicket," right at mid wicket just left of the thicket, at the right of leg gully, the wicked keeper kept wicket, the fielder at forward short leg had a short square leg (or did the fielder at short square leg have a backward long leg), the fielder at deep square leg had a short "mid wicket" or did the fielder at short mid wicket have a deep square leg), the silly mid on was very serious, the silly mid off was very delirious, the silly point made a point of being quite deleterious, the third man had a fine leg and a deep fine leg in the outfield, the fine legs dated Finns (first and second cotton slips at long on, under covers, at very deep mid wicket), the third man dated a fourth man (a Freudian slip at *Long John's* under extra covers, deep in the thicket), and while wily philatelists can lick it, when the red ball is clean-bowled or the white ball is no-balled, it's "just not very cricket, old boy" so that no lawn bowling is allowed, the footballers can't kick it, the hard-boys can't "dick it," the peasants can't "hick it," the Irish can't "Mick it," the London boys can't "nick" it, the teenagers can't "hickey" it, the spin-bowlers can't quick it, the milkmaids can't "trick-it," the peasants can't hayrick it, the workers can't "sick it," the asthmatics can't Vick it, the gate-keepers can't ticket, the candle-makers can't wick it, Jimmy "stop playing cricket with Jiminy Cricket," yet he made a wicked catch in this cricket match on the wicket pitch by the thicket patch near the cottage thatch by the cut-wheat batch front the haycock-hatch back the farm-gate latch, and let's all behave and behoove that all the overs at Over are over by afternoon tea. The grass is getting thicker and the wicket-keeper is getting quicker, the umpires are perspiring, the ladies admiring, the town-gentry squiring, April time is for drinking up dark "black-and-tans," and May time is hay-time for thinking up stark wedding "bans," June time's not for shrinking from park-cricket tans, July time is for winking at Susan Mark in the stands, August time is for linking up with disorderly fans, September time is for "mink-coating" up with flirtatious Dan's, it's all over by October time when the twilight starts to flicker, the bookmakers dicker, the un-married ladies weave wicker, the farmers' fruit-pickers pick the vegetables far quicker, some near-sighted couples leap-frog to bicker, sometimes she'll trick him and sometimes he'll kick her, some can't wait to snicker, others can't weight to eat up their Snickers, so let's all take off our "shades" and pull up our knickers, let's look up to our betters, ticket up to our bettors, when the cricket is rained-out we'll shout out "all the better," the players pull over their pullovers, pull out the "covers," the covers are pulled-over, the wicket is covered up, the pensioners sober up, the cupboards are opened, the low-rollers are roiled, the high-rollers are "rolled," the kettles are boiled, the cricket-whites are soiled, the grass-snakes remain coiled, lay your odds on at Doyle's, the *epee's* are foiled, the bar-girls seem gargoyle, the County fans are loyal, the ground-keepers toil and according to "rambling" Sid Rumpo the answer (forever) "lies in the soil." *Ad locum.*

Afternoon Tea.

Snoozing and cruising in the afternoon shade, *The Scholastic Irishman* jumped out of the frying-pan and into the *EuroGlam Eponymous* of watercress and the *belle epoque* of prawn finger-sandwiches *chacun a son gout.* on tablecloths plaid, dining on *Beef Wellington* with the Duke, on *Pavlova* cake with Anna, on *Savarin* sponge with Antoine Brillat, on *Apple Charlotte* with George III's Queen, on *Sally Lunn* teacake in the bath at Bath, on a second *Mozartkugeln* with Paul Furst, on *Garibaldi Biscuit* with Giuseppe, on *Madeleine* cake with chef Palmier, *Sachertorte* with Franz Sacher, on *Peach Melba* on Elba with Ex-Officer Escoffier and Dame Nellie, on *Melba Toast* at the Ritz, on *Chateaubriand* with Ambassador Vicomte, on *Oysters Rockefeller* with Monica, eating *The Sandwich* with the 4th Earl (what a pearl), sipping *Earl Grey* tea with the 1st Earl (what a whirl), tasting *Lady Grey* with the 2nd Earl (what a girl), tasting *Lady Grey Tea* with Pearl (what a swirl), dicking Marzipan's Dream into Lady Grey with Marquis de Sade and licking *Frangipani* cream off Lady Grey's Tea with Marquis Muzio, all the while the dear musk deer graze, the musk ducks duck in the muskeg, the fishermen lunge at the muskellunge, the Rusk-Mallon's suck on their muskmelon's, the "must-go" Jeans in their musky jeans all speak Muskogean, the musk ox box, the musk plants wilt in the silt of the Castle Vanderbilt, the musk rats bat, the dusk bats rat, the musk turtle snaps at the rows of musk roses, the *Four Musketeers* sip on their beers, *The Four Seasons* drag on, it's the sum of Vivaldi, the summer of Viyella, the Legend of King Arthur, the magic of Merlin, the vivaciousness of Lady Vivien; the vivarium enchanting with the *viva voce's* aplenty, the ravines are running with viverines of twenty, the *vivas* are over, the young children roll over in the viviparous clover, the young lovers lie bare-ass in the crab-apple grass, the old hippies fight dragons and "drag" on the "grass," the "Old Boys" swig flagons frequently and "act-out" their class, the schoolboys get nagged on for just being crass. *Post Meridiem.*

From a Maid to a Made Woman.

Now if you ever met Beckett he always said "feck it !" (and we're all very glad that his name wasn't Buckett), but the real tale was told and exclusively sold that when Beckett was clean-bowled by dirty Wilson Pickett it's alleged with a pledge that he *really* said "fuck it !" In England a gentleman can six-bowl a maiden-over at cricket but the rest of the World two-balls a maiden under the thicket ! Whether a single or double, *Oi vay, we're in trouble !* There are devoured over-laden maidens with very heavy "made" men, soured heavy-laden hand-maidens randy for dandy Quinn Aidan, bowered under-laden sea-maidens in Yemenic Aden, cow-herd milk-laden dairy-maidens in beucolic meadows, very-scary hairy maidens in petrific forests, well-endowed bare maidens in vaporific showers, well-enshrouded bower-maidens in pontific towers, cowered lady-maidens for menhaden in damnific Hades, towered milk-maidens for prolific kisser men, flowered mermaidens for trans-pacific fishermen, but only in-service, unswerving, serf-serving, serving *Himself* maidens for *our* sailor buoy, *our* arboretum bhoy, and the dark, stripling boy-Joyce becomes the bark-stripping Joyce-boy, who then makes like a tree, and leaves. *Nemini contradicente.*

Bloomsday.

He made the right turn by turning left from His mother's knee, and a left turn by serving the wrong spoon and stirring His father's tea, He appealed His relationship most celibate with a celebrated appellate, praised on an artesian paisan, prayed for a partisan artisan, He read on Byron and Shelley until they were eclipsed by the telly, He fought with His *Clann na Talmhan* with His bought-for-naught, saught-for-aught talisman displayed and replayed against the fraught Taliman (what a chopped-off hand He was dealt), yet His ameliorating Celtic health, His defoliating Zurich stealth, His diminishing Dublin wealth, His Italian Trieste tryst all Universe, in transverse got better, in traverse got worse, and that was the end of this little verse, which he sold for a song and a six-pence *sesterce.* He revered Paul Revere and his Riders, He persevered with Raul Perverse and his readers, always supported Al Davis and his Oakland Raiders, and with His deteriorating sight nursed by a private duty day-nurse, His deleterious plight worsened by a Public Health night-nurse, His discriminating bite heightened by a new-roster foster nurse, yet now even worse He had a curse on his purse which made Him accurse, He would disburse from one purse, reimburse into another purse, pre-curse from another verse, in a coarse way would curse, would write the right way inverse, would right the wrong way diverse, wrong the write way sub-verse, in His work He would submerse, His words intersperse, His car in reverse, became more perverse and much less adverse, would coerce and converse, His writings asperse, His verse more averse, had to rehearse riding the roads to Rhodes with Sir Cecil in a hearse, as He *really* thought

He would die at high noon on His own, very own *appointed*

Doomsday, an inevitable "doom and gloom" day, that "lower

the boom" day, that "bell tolls for whom" day, that "from the

womb to the tomb" day, that Addison "Ka-Boom !" day, that

"kaput and zoom" day, that "fly me 'round the moon" day, a

"new clean sweeps broom" day, that "fruit of the loom" day,

that "later not soon" day, that "you name the tune" day, on

Estonia's "Mark Poon day," on that "no Inn at the room" day,

when Joyce shouted His voice with words not very choice in

the reading room, gave up and lay down in the dressing room,

laid-up in his grave-down, paid up in the living room, grayed

up His palette in the drawing room, sated His palate in the

dining room, sprayed on His perfume in the powder room,

drank coffee in the tea room, watched the ocean from the sea

room, saw the critics in the "you see !" room, the civics never

had elbow room, the writers came from Khartoum, the dieters

dined on legumes, North African tourists and South African

Boerists all thought He would croak *until* THAT "Barnacle

the bride and Joyce the groom" day, *that* 16th of June day, that

blooming day lovers surrendered on that "soft, slow, sweet

swoon of sin" day when Henry Flower flowers bloomed *just* on

that *one-and-only* bloom-day, that dear Dublin *"Bloom's Day,"*

on that "never too soon" day that dear Leopold "the leopard" just started to Bloom day, and even Wystan Hugh Auden in his Vermont hugh garden sent a telegram with glee just after planting a tree, "bloom for the people, don't be a family shrub." *Senex nequissime.*

The Horticultural Hemingway.

Well now, on political hoardings in the Springtime sprang "Bloom for the People," and on apolitical boardings sprung again the family shrubs with the spring wine, sprang again Aubry de la Mottraye and Lady Mary Wortley Montagu who introduced the coquetry of *morning glory*, the concealed love of *acacia*, the coldness of *hortensia*, the heart's ease of *pansies*, the ingratitude of *buttercups*, the neglected beauty of *throatwood*, the dangerous pleasures of *tuberose*, the curiosity of *sycamore*, the disdain of *rue*, I am worthy of you (says the *white rose*), the perseverance of *magnolia* and the foppery of *coxcomb*. Now sprung Barnacle Nora, the pin-up of *Interflora*, pining and knitting, here a bobble, there a buttonhole, contrast a color, cast on with a flourish, a double treble crochet while dreaming of croquet, a garter stitch (in time), a quick knit slip stitch through back, let's mark a stitch, purl and pattern, pass slipped stitches over, reverse and selvedge, skein and cast on, please slip, knit and psso, pull up your stockings and stockinette stitch, yarn forward through the back loop, yarn back through the front loop, and yarn over. Now sprang Joyce James, the into Nora, wining and sitting, presenting an evergreen wreath (his lasting affection) *mina rakastan sinua*; with ten leaflets and nine berries (for nineteen years) *tha gradh agam ort*; a red rose-bud (pure and lovely) *maney tamari satey pyar che*; a twig of ivy (for friendship) *aloha i'a au oe, aloha au la o'e*; some peach-blossom (He was *her* captive) *mai tumaha pyar karta hu*; gilded with periwinkle (sweet remembrance) *mahn dousett daram, ushegheh-tam*; and bachelor's-button (love's hope) *mi-an aap say piyar karta hun*. From earnest lemmings to falling lemons, Ernest always did it Heming's Way. *O audaciam immanem.*

Pre-Consummate Erections.

The degenerate Joyce did observe that Barnacle Nora could speak Irish, English and French but didn't know how to say "no" in any of them. The bespectacled Nora did observe that juicy Joyce never made passes at girls who wore glasses, He couldn't lead her to horticulture but Dorothy Roth's-child could make her think. Nora was an ecdysiast in elastoplast, a nyphomaniac that would everlast, would disrobe so ever fast, had a body divinely cast, fly her knickers from any mast, and from her fellatio past and her experience vast, in her managerie aghast knew that brevity was the soul of lingerie. He knew that behind the rise of every successful man was a woman and she knew that behind the fall of every successful man was another woman. He fell in love with His eyes, she fell in love with her ears. He knew His clear conscience was the sign of a bad memory, while she knew that although the voices in her head were not real, she had plenty of ideas. *He* may have started the relationship by chasing *her*, but *she* was going to end it by catching *Him* ! He had two excellent theories for arguing with Nora but unfortunately neither of them worked. She knew that *anytime* she told Him to go to Hell, she could explain it with such dexterity and sincerity that by the time he figured it out He was actually looking forward to the trip ! He did an awful lot of talking but she always said that He had very little to say. Besides, no one is ever listening unless you fart. He was young enough to know that when a barrister's lips were moving, he wasn't learning much; but was old enough to know that a closed mouth gathers no foot. She knew His writing fruition would bring them attrition, but she also knew that when tempted to fight fire with fire, the Fire Department *always* used water. He knew the wine and the dine and the fine line before cuddling her, but she knew the fine line between holding Him down and not letting Him get away. Their hospitality always made their guests feel at home (while wishing they were) and always created happiness wherever they went (like their guests did whenever *they* left).

He heard voices, she saw invisible people, and they were both convinced that everyone else had no imagination whasoever. Ecclesiastical doctrine taught Him that if you give a man a fish he will eat for a day, teach him how to fish and he will never be hungry. Nora was concerned that if anybody taught Him how to fish He would sit in a boat and drink beer all day. She knew somedays she would be the dog but other days she might be the tree. Both realized they were born naked, wet and hungry, and got slapped on the bare ass, but then things got better. They got experience when they both didn't get what they wanted, but were wise enough not to take a sleeping pill and a laxative at the same time. He purchased a preshrunk, sexy, shiny-sheen, soft silk-shirt in a sale; three short, sharp swords in scabbard sheaths; and an Argyle gargoyle from Carlisle for gobbing and gobbling His gabbling goblins. She had time on her hands wishing, wanting, wailing and washing her wrought Irish wristwatch in lovely lemon-lime liniment. Her lotions and emotions ran the whole gamut from J to N but His promotions and commotions were indelibly centered on the hole-game of her yen. She was a Barnacle in a binnacle (and He would soon find out in what direction they would be going together). No longer the Paille Maille pilgrim nonchalently waiting at the gate of idleness he quietly observed her modest bodice most titillate, her genitals non-menstruate, her introate most imperforate below the *mons* protuberate which would always regenerate when reclining most prostrate. His pre-consummate date-with-a mate, His man-with-a-plan, from the fire-to-the-pan, would firstly lubricate her labiate with the utmost of luxuriate, silently penetrate, then noisily de-hyphenate, full-o-delight delightfully invaginate, concisely consumate on her cycle most ovulate, passionately impregnate her uterus proliferate, pontificate his proletariate, the lady quite incubate, perhaps a cherub twice neonate, then a time for recuperate, a Mr Joyce quite rejuvenate, a seaman with semen, no crazy agenocratia on His agenda, a situation most procreate, a consideration most proliferate, the race must be promulgate, for all the worldly populated to the delight of the Pontificate and the Royal Dublin Deity, with the admiration of the Church and the loyal Publican Society, and all this with the Marquis of Queensberry Rules being observed in all their propriety. *Optime !*

On the Royal Consummation of Nora Barnacle.

And from the ante-room to the afternoon, from assume to abloom, from be-gloom to be-plume, from catacomb to costume, from enwomb to re-Bloom, from entomb to disentomb, from inhume to illume, from reassume to resume, from pre-doom to pre-dawn there was wine to consume, and with all power to the plume, the Joyce Man suddenly sat up, barked like a young pup, of His whisky had a quick sup, of His holy water a half-a-cup, He went through his poses, sent posies of red roses to ever-longing Nora all the way from Bora Bora by way of the O'Connell Street Inter-Flora, did a Saint Vitus' dance, got an Emperor Titus advance, got up and "got it up" and *now* and *only* now did "Introitus Coitus" Joyce find His "adroitus, so it's us" voice, *then* and *only* then got His "let's go, it's us" choice, and with Nora's permission, *then* her submission, He finally finangled the Bermuda triangle, and to the sound of involuntary trumpets, He triumphantly mounted her voluntary crumpets, trumpeted voluntarily, "trumped" Donald Trump, and then voluntarily entered the glistening gates of her heavenly temple. She was a real cutey, He just grabbed on her "booty," found her cute "tutti-frutti," and then like every proud Irishman shouted out, and went in, and just "did His duty."

(Pause).

"Sainte go saol agat, Bean ar do mhian agat," said the misogynist in the midst of the latecomers delayed by the swirling Irish mist who missed the Royal Consummation. "And what does all that blather mean, you bladder ?" asked the *Quare Fella.* "Ah, sure, many years of wedded bliss to them both" smiled the white-beard, ever-feared, double-geared, never jeered, ever leered, always appeared, never queer,

prestigiously reared, royalty seered, politically seared, balcony-
tiered, writingly veneered, demonstrably weird, ageingly
yeared, benevolent Great Britain Shaw, "and I'll even put it in
the London Evening Standard for them, that I will, and more,"
says he, the multitude of one, the commotion of two, the gobble
of three, the flock of four, the hive of five, the ticks of six, the
heaven of seven, the gate of eight, the wine of nine and the
tumult of ten. "*Leanbh gach blian agat, is solas na bhflaitheas
tareis antsail seo agat !*"

Post-Consummate Affections.

Now from the abort to the long of it, the deed was done,
no longer abstinence with agreeability, but affluence
with impressibility, benevolence with acceptability,
blandiloquence with immutability, breviloquence with
impalpability, conference with amiability, common sense
with immeasurability, benificence with admirability,
competence with accountability, confidence with
impressionability, deference with amicability, diligence
with amenability, eloquence with approachability,
eminence with assimilability, equivalence with associability,
excellence with attainability, grandiloquence with
attractability, impotence with collapsibility, inconsequence
with cohesibility, incompetence with cognoscibility,

incipience with civility, indifference with commensurability, inexperience with communicability, inference with commutability, influence with comparability, innocence with compatibility, immanence invisibility, immense convincibility, imminence with venerability, incense with ascendibility, intelligence with comprehensibility, magnificence with conformability, magniloquence with credibility, munificence with creditability, non-residence with demonstrability, nescience with culpability, omiscience with curability, obedience with dispensability, omnipotence with docibility, His continence with her adorability, opulence with durability, quantivalence with affability, permanence with educability, pre-eminence with eligibility, preference with enunciability, providence with equability, penitence with desirability, percipience with memorability, plenipotence with hereditability, prepense with expansibility, prescience with computability, prevalence with perceptibility, reverence with fallibility, reference with feasibility, salience with febrility, residence with flexibility, redolence with sensibility, resilience with tranquillity, self-confidence with fluctuability, self-defence with formidability, sense with fragility, somnolence with gentility, subservience with gracility, super-eminence with humility, succulence with describability, His plume-essence became detumescence, and His man-scent, man sent.

Ardens in cupiditatibus.

Post-Communion Reflections.

Now from the thong to the short of it, the dame was done, her deflowered essence became re-Blooming sense, no accidence of absorbability, no coincidence of accessibility, commence with much agility, condense with much proclivity, His circumference with her capability, His concupiscence with her acquirability, their confluence, her dilatability; the consequence, her conceivability; no defence hostility for His offense fertility, a convenience with irreparability, no difference answerability, no diffidence tactility, dense exchangeability, disobedience with revocability, dissidence with wincurability, dispense satiability, evidence incontestability, exigence delectability, expedience irretrievability, expense deductibility, immense orgiasticity, flatulence with dissolvability, flocculence with excitability, frankincense with fusibility, impenitence with indefensibility, impertinence with incorrigibility, impudence with contemptibility, fraudulence without retractability, improvidence in the form of despicability, incidence with imperfectibility, incoincidence with inexorability, incongruence with deplorability, incontinence with compressibility, inconvenience with irresponsibility, indolence with distensibility, inexpedience with detestability, insipience with descendibility, insolence with corrigibility, intense with corruptibility, irreverence with intangibility, malefience with perturbability, malevolence with punishability, mellifluence with scurrility, negligence with dissolubility, pertinence with damnability, pestilence with gullibility, pretense with viability, prurience with deceptibility, recompense with errability, reticence with perishability, sub-tense with alienability, suspense indigence with impregnability, tense with refutability, thence with nihility, truculence and hostility, turbulence and temptability, vehemence and ignobility, violence and incivility, virulence and futility, whence indocility, hence exhaustibility, their corpulence contractility, no longer a Doctor of Divinity to patrol in this vicinity, and her woman-scent, Heaven sent. Their consummation was their communion, and neither of them missed it, unless they were having it. *Ipse Dixit.*

Spiritual Awakening.

The whole literary World literally shook the dust off it's books, grabbed their coats off their hooks, re-hired their cooks, fired the crooks, finessed their looks, came out of their nooks, went into the *Suq's,* moved all their rooks, took single boxes for their dates, took two single foxes on dates, dated three toy-boys on horses, ate four dinner-courses, placated five coarse diners, reviewed six oil-well refiners, tended seven drunk-driving victims in Heaven, invented a method at home for home-alone attics to never give eight methadones to home-alone addicts, would hate to bury crematory ashes in Haight-Ashbury cemeteries, nine lives for the dog, and "ten out of ten" for the phrasal and sentential semantics of the nasal and sentimental romantics from Lord Baden Powell with his Kenya-made trowel, to the always enhancing and hallways enchanting, bade the ink-laden *plume de ma tante* to become the pink-maiden *plume de mon Bloom.* When now greeted with "good evening" he could explain why it wasn't, when one careless match could start a forest fire he could explain how it takes a whole box to light a campfire, He believed anyone who told Him there were four billion stars but He *always* checked when told the paint was wet. A bus stops at the bus station, a train stops at the train station but now nothing stopped at His work station. He could get a loan from any bank as He could now prove He didn't need it. He started to borrow money from pessimists as He knew they wouldn't expect it back. He knew money couldn't buy happiness, but it sure made misery easier to live with. He once lent a friend $ 20, never saw them again, but felt it was well worth it. He realized He needed a parachute to skydive, as a honey bee needed a hive, but if stung by a sky-diving honey bee, he didn't need honey anymore, and in sky-diving, he soon reasoned, if at first you don't succeed, skydiving is not for you. He was never plagued with plagiarism (He never stole from anybody), but now he could steal words from anyone (and call it research). He was a plenium in a vacuum. Joyce's joy was always Finnegan, with his bow-tie tied up to his chin again, who always bowed low down to his shin again, and made a very high vow never to sin again, and now the Re-Joyce was fun again, Father Dunnigan was done again, and with great allegory rejoice, the Tate Gallery Re-Joyce, with white-lightening striking the chiming Church spire, enlightening and hiking His pen-ultimate attire, He recruited Reuters, addressed the Associated Press, re-ignited United Press International, and was published immediately by reporters wire ! His Ulysses *now* seen by overseers overseas, *NOW* the Artist without poor traits, *NOW* the Old Man with Portraits, He *now* sprinted out into the fun-in-the-sun with the Dubliners, *now* became all-at-one-again in the rain with the Publiners, *now* heard again the "hurrah's" from across the Curragh and the "aaragh's" from up the Borough, He *now* admired the horse's furrow down in the Vale of Tullough, He had awoke from His ill-timed illegitimate and pill-time illiterate amnesiestical stroke to his Yen, and with a well-timed legitimate and quill-time literate amnestic stroke of His pen, manipulated a portable handheld communications transcriber to stencil, capitulated a sortable foothold communion perscriber

113

to pencil, ate a quick bowl of peas and a lentil, watched Barbra Streisand's film Yentyl, got a prescription for Bentyl, passed Hid exams dental, handled Nora most gentle and decided to scribe in a manner most mental. Now with quiet post-consummate glee, from a *Summa Cum Laude* tea to a quiet summer-*cum* glee, a victorious Valedictorian with a V-sign, a Poet Laureate by design, an Einstein divine, a prophecy Celestine, a great Constantine, a modern-day Frankenstein, a Frank with a stein, watched Frank and Stein, a Frank with sense, an incensed Frank with Myrhh, a drunk without a cent, gave up the "moonshine" and May wine, Colleens and *poteen,* got Tommy Smythe and Sonny Smith to smash tureens into smithereens, gave up the night whine and day wine, altar wine and table wine, red wine and white wine, sparkling wine and turpentine, apple wine and cider wine, and after a very short while with the Bishop of Argyll, said three *Our Father's* for our mothers, ten *Hail Mary's* for Mary, and like the irreligious and non-apostolic swine, got out of line and drunkenly rendered a new version most aversion in un-rhyming time, sang loudly and lustfully, beautifully and bust-fully, and before the barman shouts "time !" would sing one more time, for all the good old times, the good old days of one's youth, the bad young nights of two's long-ago couth, that New Year's Eve "goldie," that *Hogmanay* oldie, a hootenanny version of the new *Auld Lang Syne.*

The Count, The State, and the State of the Irish Counties.

Now that was not in any way unusual for any one of the many *Dubliners,* any Dub-man and Pub-man, Cork man and pork-man, dinner-knife and fork man, Paddy-man and Daddy-man, Mick-man and milkman, Kerry man and Derry man, *Danny-Boy* and "fanny" boy, Wild Colonial Boy and tame conjugal man, every Adare man with a dare, every Limerick man with a limerick, any man who had ever "done a gal" from Donegal or made maid Mona moan in County Monaghan, don't ask Mary Monaghan about maids moaning in Mall Ala Moana, the awfully old men in Offaly chase lonesome doves in the groves, pace lonely dears around their stoves, mace woodland deers in the forests yet are "never too old" for the Offaly old ladies. Now in County "Mayo-hold the cheese" sandwiches are not for the poplar adventurous with snow feet in County Westmeath but are for the popular edentulous with no teeth in Meath. In Antrim the English entomologists are chasing ants but the American gynecologists are *always* chasing "trim," *Your Man* never gave up the chase after chasing eclairs with dear chaste Claire in Clare, laid Lady Lois Lowe low in Laois then laid low in Laidlow, trimmed Oh My Lei's *lei* in Leitrim, went "all the way" the Gaul's way on the causeway in Galway, had a "sly go" in Sligo; a firm man (agh !) in Fermanagh is good to find, *A Good Man Is Hard To Find* wrote Flannery O'Connor, a hard man is good to find says Connie O'Flaherty, and just to prove them all right, the Protestants are always "getting it up" in County Down. Now the arm-less, harmless army of Armagh ladies always keep count at tea, keep Count de Tyrone at arm's length, and wouldn't Dr Kildare kill any dare anyway, whichever way scare, take time to care, ride on his mare, whether clothed or bare, not pay the fare, rearrange his hair, fire his gun at a hare, scare a fox from its lair, or better a pair, went on a tear, turned up anywhere and like Spring-Heeled Jack (the Marquis of Waterford), would fly over the shack, would never look back, and with incredible knack, make a sound like a "quack" and scare the *bejabbers* into anybody and out of everybody else ! Democrat Al Gore with wife Tipper Rary Gore, after getting am-Bush-ed in Florida, got gored by a bull in a China Shop in Tipperary, very scary, but in Castlerock's Rock Ridge the cattle are raped and the women stampeded (stranger than diction). The car-riding O'Mata Mexicans ride "low riders" in Carlow, the Yorkshire Terriers stride east in West Riding, guide west in East Riding, the swans glide south in the Winter, the "Hunt" gallops north in the Summer depsite icicles and bicycles, and have it on record that they n'er hit a runner ! In Kilkenny they fight cats and kill Kenny, in Waterford they can afford water but not ford

116

water or fiords, in Longford it doesn't take long to ford water or fjords but they can't afford water, in Kerry they're merry, count many a common man called Ross is especially common in County Roscommon, and many a man-with-a-plan for a woman-with-a-pan was told "down Patrick !" in Downpatrick or told to keep his Wick Glow Energy at "wick low" in Wicklow. Though chastised for a vexed word in Wexford, a County Cork "screw" is not about corkscrews, yet most suprisingly, nobody has *ever* confessed to the Mouth of the Shannon. *Peccavimus. Improbissimum vero libellum scripsimus.*

The Inaugural Meeting .... (Play the Second).

On the Inaugural Meeting of the Anglo-Irish Diabolical Dublin Debating Society (financed by *Aid for AIDDDS* or synonym for Gomer's Odyssey) was called to order on the third *De Ceadaoin* of *Meitheamh* in the year two, two noughts and a four by Aston Villa's Deon Dublin (flying the flag of St. George) in the Afton Villa Neon Dublin (flying the flag of St. Patrick) situated up and to the right on John Bull's other Island. Firstly, an English Delegate got up and read the British Riot Act. "Our Sovereign Lord the King chargeth and commandeth all ye persons, being assembled here, to immediately disperse yourselves, and peacefully depart this habitation or take off to their lawful businesses, upon the pains

117

contained in the Act made in the year 1714, that being the first year of the reign of King George the First for preventing tumults and riotous assemblies. God Save the King." (Pause for risibility, jocundity and blitheness from the Irish-Anglos). Secondly, an Irish Magistrate got up and read the Irish Code Duello of 1777. "The first offense requires the first apology, and hopefully the retort is more offensive than the insult, the aggresor to beg pardon in express terms. All blows are strictly prohibited between Gentlemen as no verbal apology can be received for such an insult, especially after the parties have taken their ground. Any insult to a lady under a Gentleman's care or protection is to be considered, as by one degree, a greater offense than if given to the gentleman personally, and to be regulated accordingly. Challenges are not to be rendered after dark, unless the party to be challenged intends leaving the place of offense before morning. Seconders are bound to attempt a reconciliation before the meeting takes place, any conflict to agitate the nerves and make the hands shake will end the business for this day. (Pause for giggling, snickering, sniggering, tittering, guffawing, yukking, chortling, chuckling, cackling, cachinnating, roaring and shrieking from the Anglo-Irish). Spokesman for the English Descendency in Ireland was Malcolm S. Forbes (intermittent, disinterested, impolite applause) whose notables included John Millington Synge,

Samuel Beckett, Oliver Goldsmith, Jonathan Swift, and William Butler Yeats, to name just a few. Spokesman for the Irish Ascendency in England was James Joyce (tumultuous welcome, standing ovation, deafening applause) whose quotables included Flan O'Brien, Patrick Kavanagh, Brendan Behan, Sean O'Casey, Oscar Wilde and George Bernard Shaw, to name a few of the many. "And for more decades than London politicos like to remember, Ireland's (literary might) has been making and unmaking British parliaments and Prime Ministers" commenced the Scottish Forbes, instantaneously turning the Protestant hordes into threatening swords. (*Them's fightin' words* mumbles the Quare Fella) as the clamorous, clandestine, Cameron Clan intone *chlanna nan con thigibh a so's gheibh sibh feoil* to witch the shaking spears of the Britannia clan replies "Otay ebay, orway otnay otay ebay: atthay isway ethay estionquay: Etherwhay 'istay oblernay inway ethay indmay otay uffersay Ethay ingsslay andway arrowsway ofway outrageousway ortunefay, Orway otay aketay armsway againstway away easay ofway oublestray, andway ybay opposingway endway emthay ?" Retorted James Joyce "and this lovely land that always sent, her writers and artists to banishment, and in the spirit of Irish fun, betrayed her leaders, one by one," clandestinely burning Protestant words of the detonating Lords (*sad but true, glad but due, bad to rue, mad to sue, tad to crew, had to view* rumbles the Quare Fella). "Now, now, lads" says Conor Cruise O'Brien "Irishness is not primarily a question of birth or blood or language; it is the condition of being involved in the Irish situation, and usually being mauled by it." (*And the Irish keen Keane's keel-hauled to Australia, the fierce men wheel-called to Monserrat, the Pearse women balled in Yankee halls by American Patriots, black-balled in swanky malls by African polyglots, the children walled-in by the Romans, sent out to Africa by the* Dail, *welcomed in France by* De Gaulle, *the priests were appalled, and all the unwanted and unwashed dumped off in Youghal,* humbles the Quare Fella). "Gentlemen, gentlemen," sighs Lydia M. Child "we all know the Irish writers with their glowing hearts and reverent credulity are desperately needed in this cold age of intellect and skepticism." (*but the old skeptical intellects abide in England and can't possibly be compared to the bold intellectual skeptics who thrive in Ireland* grumbles the Quare Fella). "Ladies, ladies, laddies, lassies, ladles and gadflies" says James Connolly "the Irishman in English literature may be said to have been born with an apology in his mouth." (*Ah, but it is the Englishman in Irish literature who wishes he was born with all that verbal ventriloquy in his head,* tumbles the Quare Fella). "Cum, cum, ladies turn" interjects Edna O'Brien "here's what I reply when

120

anyone asks me about the Irish character. I say look at the trees. Maimed, stark and misshapen, but ferociously tenacious." (*More like the wild bees*, bumbles the Quare Fella, *tamed, dark and mistaken, but tenaciously ferocious*). "Now, now, Patricks and Colleens, Bartholomews and Fionas, we all acknowledge that the Irish are a fair people, always proven by the fact that they never speak well of one another" blurts out Samuel Johnson. (*The blithering spalpeen, the blathering spaldeen*, dumbells the Quare Fella, *and whose "fair" people are you rambling and gambling about anyway ? Some Fair people work the swings, the big wheel and the roundabouts, they aren't fair but are dark, they're unfair to the employed and we call then the "tinkers." Other fair people work stings, the big steal and are lager-louts, they work in the dark and are unfair, they're always unemployed and we call them the "drinkers." Now some fair people aren't unfair, don't work at The Fair, are employed and are fair, they build wings, small wheels and just barge-about, whether they're dark or they're fair, fair or unfair, work unfair at The Fair, always pay their fare, they're really unemployable derelicts and so we call them the "thinkers"*). "Come now," retorts Johnson "I am not a Jester to be paraded before the King nor a eunuch to be paraded before the Queen ......" (but they were *ALL* on him now)......"you're Merry Andrew to Henry VIII, Berdic to William the Conqueror, Will Somers at

121

Hampton Court, Yorick to the Court of Denmark and Aksakoff to Czarina Elizabeth" chant the apostolic Catholics. "You're Adelsburn to King George I, Patison to Thomas More, 'Cardinal' Soglia to Pope Gregory XVI, Abgely to Louis XIV, Rosen to Maximilian I, thanks-a-million too, Patche to Cardinal Wolsey, Colquhoun to Mary Queen of Scots, and Da'gonet to King Arthur, pant the ameliorating Protestants. "Lighten up, boys" murmurs Peggy Noonan in her odorous monotone (like gas from a burner) "the Irish are often nervous about having the appropriate face for the occasion. They have to be happy at weddings, which is a strain, so they get depressed; they have to be sad at funerals, which is easy, so they get happy," (*and at least Finnegan's awake* crumbles the Quare Fella) bowing respectfully as William Butler eats at the MCA and drops two "why's" before afternoon tea, bee-hive snobbing "a poet is by the very nature of things ....." and is unceremoniously and immediately upstaged downtown by the very poet (Joyce) that the butler William personally named *The Scholastic Irishman* who now know-how starts sobbing "a poet is by the very stature of wings who thrives with satire insincerity, or blather, to the bettor his artistry, the more in sense here his wife. His strife is a sediment in dying and those who went before him have a left to mow it. Under everything, it is un-necessary that the empiric poet's sight be shown, that

122

the wee-us could misunderstand that his idolatry is *nae* a rooting weed but the screech of a woman; that is, a right object to perceive something in any part, to band apart forceps five many fears, too wet to woo a bath three no t'other Maid Gonne has gone, to refuse two's own wrought when the noughts of mothers mass the paucity of the moon in front of it .... to take another's wife deep well of tree's herbs (witch are so much further from one's bowl) to the wit-some of the spoiled." (This left pour BMW Yeats foaming at the mouth, roaming in the south, combing at his gout, droning with a clout, honing with a flout, groaning with a pout, loaning for the grout, moaning at the joust, cloning of a mouse, and intoning 'folks is queer as nowt' while Citizen Kane claims that "anybody who believes in fairies is mad" even though *everyone* who believes in Mary's is glad). At this moment, George Moore stands up to make a speech. "My one claim to originality among Irishmen it that I have never made a speech...." he starts off.... (w*ell, don't start now* tumbles the Quare Fella, *and the less we hear from Moore the better*) ! "Well now, it's all coming out now, here and now, there now, isn't it now ?" upspake wild Oscar "cause we coarse Irish are too poetical to be poets; we are a nation of brilliant (successes), and the greatest talkers since the Greeks !" (*And we are too literary to be writers; we are a nation of scintillant excesses and the greatest shiters since the Romans, themselves a* *nation of diapers wiping their asses in front of the Trojan blighters who stick their tongues out at the Greeks who are barefoot in the park, stuck in the mud, soaked to the kin, and can't stop the rain with their window-shield wipers,* jumbles the Quare Fella). "It is often said that in Ireland there is an excess of genius un-sustained by talent; but there is talent in the tongues" intercedes V. S. Pritchett (*the very silly sod* fumbles the Quare Fella, *any auld sod can see the talented geniuses in the tall tents in The Round, the heinous talent of the wall gents in the Four Courts, the gallant Fenians on the Dail bench, the malevolent mean Ann's of the hall dents, the rampant Armenians of the pall vents, whatever, etc*). "Yet a people so individual in it's genius, so tenacious in love or hate, so captivating in it's nobler moods" admiringly states F. E. Smith, Lord Birkenhead (*and we're all drinking down the Guinness in Hartlepool, Liverpool, Blackpool and Dorset's Poole, that's for sure*, adds the Quare Fella). At that point stood up the latest, greatest, noble Nobel Laureate from Mossbawn, born one Seamus Heaney (pronounced "shame-us he-knee"). "Now Ireland is where strange tales begin and happy endings are possible...." he starts off before being interrupted by the schlock, gimcrack, gin-*craic*, chintzy, tatty haughty-taughty, that Baalem from Bedlam, the bought Charlie Haughey (pronounced "haw-hee" which is really a donkey talking backwards). "Well, now, what's

124

this all about now, here now, right now, here-and-now" says the former *an Taoiseach,* now about in his non-prime minister, sinister tea-squawk "and I'd like to think........" *"That's impossible !"* screams the non-adornful, ever scornful, cheeringly derisive and derisively cheering crowd (*and that's the very truth* yells the never-boring, goal-scoring, ever-touring Quare Fella, *and isn't it very strange that haughty Charlie owns a castle and an island and there's them in the Ghaeltacht that don't even have the electricity ! Now that's a very unhappy tale with a very strange ending) !* "Ah, but an Irishman's heart is nothing but his imagination" concludes Great Britain's Shaw (*and an Englishman's fart is nothing butt his exsanguination*) concludes the *Quare Fella* to prodigious, capacious, Brobdingnagian, magnanimous, felicitous and gratuitous applause. "I propose to bring Bill into Parliament and deprive all of you who wish to publish these theses and subject you all to peculiar penalties" concluded Lord John Campbell. All *Exit.*

Audience Response (Critics Corner).

Well, now, to put it as simple and briefly as possible, the Anglo-Irish Dublin Diabolical Debating Society spontaneously degenerated into a delirium of noise cacophonical, culture aboriginal, Hamilton Academical, smell agricultural, meaning allegorical, language alphabetical, design analytical, parts anatomical, choirs angelical, next year it's annual, each day chronological, the music classical, the weather climatical, the ambience collegial, the language colloquial, the communion communal but only after the confessional, the lesson very congregational but only after the meeting congressional, the rules constitutional, the veneer cosmetical, the sneers conflagrational, the Irish all conversational and very demoniacal, the English all corporeal and exquisitely diplomatical, the writings bureaucratical, never apologetical, findings archeological, buildings architectural, accounts arithmetical, vitriol arsenical, taste ascetical, speeches never apologetical, feelings contradictional, breathing asthmatical, signs astrological, air atmospherical, drinks very bacchanal, prayers basilical, readings biblical, speakers bibliographical, speeches bibliomaniacal, plants and flowers botanical, roast-beef very cannibal, coast-reef very nautical, ghost-leaf very funereal, the blessing very canonical, and led by the Cardinal it turned into a carnival with filings categorical, fillings dietetical, fingers didactical, and who made the rule that the rules were un-ethical? *Sine qua non.*

Religious Indoctrination.

The retired Sir Alex Douglas-Hume traveled down from Ilfracombe, his trolling Rolls Royce re-tired in the gloom, his mobile filled with Mobil by the alpha-beta-gamma fraternity in Mobile, Alabama, and in his under-tall overalls observed the English to be Episcopal and mostly quite vicarial, the Irish Druidical and mostly quietly vesperal, the Jesuits madrigal and nicely *Provencale*, the Franciscans magical and enticingly provisional, the Dominicans ecclesiastical and invitingly sabbatical, the Presbyterians denominational and very egoistical, the Baptists devotional and very egotistical, the Hugenots descensional and very inquisitorial, the Lutherans devotional and very inspirational, the Methodists Eucharistical but not very etymological, the Unitarians eulogistical but not very ethnological, the Catholics unintentional, very professional, and quite umbilical; the Protestants unmentionable, very un-professorial and quite anal; the Calvinists scriptural but not very sculptural, the Monarchists hypocritical and mostly theological, and the Republicans hysterical and mostly theoretical. He found the peasants pastoral, their leaders despotical, the hard-liners digressional, the Bard-minders discretional, the card-binders impersonal, the guard-finders dogmatical, the voices equally vocal (or is that equivocal), that's very guttural but not very grammatical, the arm-waving gestural, the seed-sowing germinal, the reed blowing pneumatological, the bead-sewing symbolical but not very symmetrical, the deed-knowing imperial but not very juridical, the feed-crowing continual but not very medicinal, the heed-towing signs logical but not very mechanical, the lead-mowing man herbal but not very germinal, the mead-glowing woman verbal but always irrational, the arboreal gerbil most biological, the Vicar in the Vickery very volitional, the wicker in the vestiges very vestigial, the snicker in the knackery very visional, the Patriarch very patronal, the Matriarch very polygonal, the terrestrial fog very zodiacal, the territorial dog very zoological, the posturing Hannibal all very mechanical, the fostering Babylonical all very rhetorical, and in the midst of the mist the physiologist most Pharisaical, the phrenologist pharmaceutical, the philologist philanthropical, the philosopher physiological, the philanthropist philological, the pharmacist phrenological, the pharmacist phthisical, the Pharisee philosophical, and now that it's finished its decidedly comical. *Schadenfreude.*

Now Published Author, Not Un-Published Pauper.

And now with the debate over, and rolled in sedate clover, without any reason and throughout every season, whether by treason and three-some, Joyce re-started re-writing again, re-breathing and re-fighting, rejoicing and re-Joyce-ing, re-voicing and re-rhyming, re-timing with *bon*-treason and re-trying with *mal*-feasance, at His landlord took a poke for making Him broke, watched poor Padraic Colum's solemn column go up in columns of solemn smoke, in the bath had a soak, became a "born-again" bloke, He quote as He spoke, He drank lemonade and Coke, enjoyed the *craic* but never impaled a bespoke, enjoyed the "crack" but never inhaled the smoke, cracked many a non-meaningful joke, smacked the back of a lager-full "moke," jogging-track walked with SMU running back Walker Doak, plighted His troth and placated His yolk, was always seen mumbling "there's 'owt queer as folk," and forthwith got Hence IVth the Chiropractor to get the crease and the grease out of His neck, the crimp and the gimp out of His limp, the spasms and phantasms out of His back, separated the men from the boys, the W.R.E.N.S. from the buoys, the Glasgow Rangers ploys from the Parkhead Celtic bhoys, the play-pens from the toys, and with a wave of His hand, an encore from the band, a cheer throughout the land, from a pre-pubic protest-ional to a near-sighted grotesque-ional, from a lonely processional to a gleaming professional, a constitutional institutional, an elocutional evolutional, a substitutional circumlocutional, now liberated from the confessional, a sinful ablutioner, a merciless executioner, a New Year's resolutioner, an atypical revolutioner, writing never-written prose like no-ever writing pro's could do so before Him, the eternalist journalist, the public adored Him, the critics deplored Him, the philanthropists ignored Him, nobody knows the Worldly pain of the stream of interrupted consciousness like *He* knows the celestial delight of the river of un-interrupted unconsciousness, like water streaming from a hose, coryza flowing from the nose, high praise indeed for His penmanship deeds, His admirers heaped praises on Him from *their* heads to *His* toes, *now* a life well worth living on the lively banks of the Liffey, courting lovely-lady lawyers in the garden-shady Law Courts, dialing slovenly Slovenian politicians in the hall of the clovenly Bohemian *Eireann Dail*, fighting *Sinn Fein* over their fine sins, attended the Republican IRA day, made His American IRA pay, let Ira have her way, let Ida have her say, visited likeable Almira, leggy Elmira, "Mistress of the Dark" Elvira, lovable Lyra, titillating, terrific Thyra; and mitigating, magnificent (my pal) Myra; all at once, all the while, in the bunny-full, tummy-full, yummy-full, funny-full, gunny sack-ful, honey-full, money-full, nunnery-full, runny-full, sunny-full dessert called Palymyra. Let the politicians make hay, to the farmers said "Hey," and most of all poetically left the *Fianna Fail* politically, became very urbanical, extremely mechanical, absolutely tyrannical, exclusively botanical, studied Brahmanical, was never charlatanical, lit His home most galvanical, and completed His ledgers at the utmost of panicle. He always thought that forlorn lady aviators always bought a place in the cockpit, but the furloughed RAF navigators always sought a plaice in the cock pit; He opposed transvestite Jay, "alternative lifestyle" Ray, lesbians like "lets-be-friends" Fay, never understood lexicon like a "lay" with a "gay," was never gay with a layman, never laid with a "gay" man, never "made" with a lesbian, knew a maid who was "gay," a happy maiden from Aden who was laughing and gay, a snappy "made" man from Leyden who was chaffing all day; supported the R.N.L.I.'s "May Day !" calls but aborted the Communist May-Day Balls, always went the wrong way when told "no it's this way," always went the right way when told "there is no way," when told "No !" He would neigh, when it was free He would pay, but would have plenty to say on that ebullient day when he was incredibly pleased to be given the "key to the Keys" when visiting "The Old Man" Hemingway "and the Sea" on East Florida's West Key. *Memento mori.*

Pre-Retirement Annual Lectures (A Confucian Analectual).

He was a gimp with a gamp, Forrest Gump with a lamp, but no hippopotomonstrosesquippedaliophobic. He would awake with the lark at the end of the dark, would alight in the light for partaking of extra parking, every week sipping weak Earl Grey morning-tea at the Duke of Earl's palatial palace-place, every noon-time kipping with Lady Earl Grey in early Greek cottages with Latter-Day wattages, every post-noon tipping busty-blonde waitresses and crusty white-coated waiters who *never* knew the difference between Irish Tayto crisps (which are chips) and chips (which are French fries), every early-afternoon whipping up soda-bread which was never so dead as not to need soda, so every late afternoon was spent snobbing with the well-breds, gobbing on the swell breads, bobbing with the apple-heads, hobnobbing with the newly-weds, yobbing with the Liverpool "reds," jobbing with the hotel beds, mobbing with the modern "Teds," robbing roofs of smolten leads, downing pints at "Donkey Ned's," lobbing pill-jars full with pharmacy meds, and then sobbing with the "low downs" up on the high downs and jogging with the "high-ups" down on the low mounds in auld County Down. He watched the bare-foot gossoons playing *camogie* on the shores of Lake Okefenokee, was a wily fox aound the green witch from Greenwich, went fishing for humuhumunukunukuapuaa after taking a quick piddle in the deep middle of Lake Chargoggagoggmanchauggagoggchaubunagungamaugg, went slurping strong Irish Tea at the edge of the sea, burping weak Florida lemonade all the way down the promenade, noisily farting with pen-ultimate glee, removing His tie, admiring your tie, drinking a "my-tai," playing chess to a tie; which was always considered the best way, man, when train-spotting a highwayman or game-slotting a low-way woman, or in the usual way at the end of the day just enjoying the usual nibby-jibby, nicknackatory, niddle-noddle, nieve-nieve-nick-nack, niminy-piminy, nipperty-tipperty, tuzzimuzzy of the Tathagatagarbha; the tetragrammation of Yahweh, the zenzizenzizenzic of the Yezdegerdian,

the anaglyphic of the Yajnavalkya, eating gefilte fish and

pfefferkuchen, a derriere-Perrier, an arriere-pensee, there was

never any other way for a non-Neanderthal neanimorphist

without philosophico-psychological phronemophobia, a

planomaniac with Pindaric pleniloquence, a non-pseudo-

anti-disestablishmentarianist with no parthenophobia for

sarmassophobes, the eternality of the omphaloepsistic omnist,

a sacred sacramentarianist, an English rapparee with Irish

repartee, a Welsh leek with a leak, spoke a varying *cynhanedd* in

a *cywydd* buying Welsh squids with English *quids,* the Scottish

bairns belting the leprechaun Irish kids with garbage-can lids to

the delight of the Yids amongst the wholesale bids in the stores

and the yacht-sailing and the retailing Sids in the *eisteddfod* at

Llanfairpwllgwyngyllgogerychwyrndrobwllllantysiliogogogoch

after first-time visiting the church of St Mary, dozing in a

hollow of white hazel, bathing in a rapid whirlpool, first-time

praying in St Tysilio's church by the red cave. He was a clap-trap

catoptomanticist, a rat-a-tat romanticist of such an assertive

asaphoialiac, a hedonic boustrophedon, a *jeunesse doree*

with juvenile jouissance, an agathokakological ashotogical,

an analytical Anacreon, an articulate anthropopithecus, a

preterpluperfect Priscillianist prefect in the Prefecture, a master

of mataeotechny, a megacephalous non-mechanomorphist, the

Metternichian of the Matterhorn, a mysterious mystagogue running rings around the Nibelungeniled, an East Indian mlechchha, a Russian muzhik, certainly no crying Abderian in Democritus's democracy, who else would query Quetzalcoatl's coat or face down a rhombicosidodecahedron ? A poor luck Porlockian in Coleridge's train of thought, Kubla Khan or Kubla can't, He contemplates the Universe yet cannot master a mistress at the Fair, or how to rescue a damsel in distress unaware, yet the caterpillar becomes a butterfly and masters the mystery of the air, when it waves it's wings in Africa it can create a hurricane in Asia, a one inch worm contemplates a continent, all entombed on a planet where the dinosaurs are extinct and the cockroaches thrive, the mosquitoes bite and the honeybees hive, the Holy Grail un-veiled, the un-Holy chalice veiled, all this going on while parakeets perch on the porch, Alabama geeks lurch in the Porsche, and the soft-setting sun glides o'er the oft-wetting tides, the Night Maiden climbs astride her white winged-horse, her robe a scarlet sunset, her eyes a fading hue, the skies a shimmering blue, she gently breezes into the crimson-filled skies, her trailing veils dancing to the setting-sun sounds, the ebb tides outgoing while the ocean tides pound, and the water-full waterfalls cascade over the white-walled tires on the tiled white walls of the wide purple parapet of Grand Cayman's quay. *Floruit.*

Wearying for the Emerald Isle.

He invented, wrote, quote and spoke of "aw-shucks" Buck
Mulligan, if Finnegan was fun again then Mulligan was
hypothesis null again, but the Joyce hypothetical thesis mulled
a twin brother, the one playing ice hockey was seen as Puck
Mulligan, the other the actor was *also* Puck Mulligan but seen
again in Mid Summer's Night's dream, but the seam never split
so auld Buck was called Chuck Mulligan at mealtimes, Cluck
Mulligan feeding the chickens, Duck Mulligan when feeding
the swans at Coole, "duck" Mulligan when feeding the bats,
Muck Mulligan on the farm, Mick Mulligan in the pub, Pluck
Mulligan when preparing the turkey, "Aw Shucks" Mulligan
on the ranch, Yuk ! Yuk ! Mulligan when watching Barney the
Flintstone, Suck Mulligan as a baby, Truck Mulligan on the
highway, Friar Tuck Mulligan in the Seminary, Luck Mulligan
in the casino, Zuruck Mulligan in Germany, Ruck Mulligan
playing rugby for the London Irish, but in Ulysses overseas in
France "if you please" was always *double entendre,* handsome,
rib-eye steak, *uber mensch* Buck Mulligan who *always* swore
that the red-heads "buck like billie-goats" and the wed-heads
"fuck like billy-goats," so without "mooning" or "spooning,"
no further ado, goodbye to Sue, what a two-do, a French street
to *rue,* good on you *blue*, a room with a view, and now back
to Eireann's green Isle, Dublin's mean style, Jim Nabors'

135

neighbors and sweet Gomer Pyle. *Seo libh canaidh Amhran na bhFiann.*

The Prodigal's Return to Auld Eireann (Part the Second).

He was always enthralled when making "last call" amongst the best and worse *Clann na Publachtas*, while walking the halls amongst the zest and terse *Clann na Dublachta*s, while dancing at Balls amongst the Press and Pearse *Clann na Republachta*s, never no time to rejoice nor no rhyme for to boast, have a cup of tea and some toast, He Mizen Head-headed for the Connemara coast, His manuscript to post, this literary ghost was never a host for a celebrity "roast" but always a candidate for an overseas post, and although His writing asyndeton made Him appear a literary simpleton, He was de-valued, de-valance-d, de-valet-ed, de-valiance-d, de-validated, and de-valor-ed by Eamon de Valera, the "Long Fellow" in Ireland; he was demoted, de-moat-ed, de-motel-ed, de-motet-ed, de-motif-ed, de-motivated, de-motley-ed, de-motored, de-mottled, de-motto-ed by "Aye, mon" the Valiant, the Longfellow in England. He went on to assize for a prize, attest at a test, did agree to a degree, got notification of his certification, was awarded an award that said "honorable mention" (quite

unlike *this* poor pauper with a dis-honorable non-mention)
and despite dystrophy of walk and atrophy of talk, became
an authoritative author, a newspaper reporter, a magazine
re-writer, a paperback "one-nighter," witnessed the daring-
do's and daring deeds of Icarious Dedalus, experienced
the fried-herring "do's" and un-caring needs of vicarious
Bloom, who as a dutiful Jew was never-ever seen with
Rosary Beads but could ever-aver be seen with *Shachen
Tov* Rosie Meads, she could ever-never keep clean from
his wet, sweaty kneads, he would come and go in her house
Chabad Chanukah "as you please," would *cum* and flow
with a "happy ending" to her *Vaad Hakashrus* tease, she was
"made in the shade" on her dry house-maid's knees, it was
all over by *Hannukah* with consummate ease, Bloom ended
up Dan Rather short-winded blueish (with a wheeze) on the
"made" house-maid made disgustingly glueish (leave-as-
much-DNA-as-you-please), and for all his blooming defaults
the depleted Bloom became very rueish, was attacked by the
shrewish, went to repent in a synagogue Jewish, which was
recently built in a suburb brand-newish, near the Temple
nexus in Temple, Texas, and then was confrontationally
asked in a manner most truish, in a *B'nai B'rith* voice
clueish, arising quite *Mitzvah* from the adjoining pewish,
"are you a Menorah mouse?" *Oi, gevald !*

Ulysses Penned at Last !

At this point He *himself* made a point of Joyce-pointing His finger, voice-pointing his Singer, conjoining His zingers, and set out on His own to reclaim His *own* throne, wrote home from *His* Odyssey and for ten adventure-full years wiped away indenture-paid tears, re-adjusted His gears, drank many beers, rutted up many young dears and hunted down many old deers, put aside His endearing fears, never listened to what He hears, ate all His corn flakes but never bothered at all with the corny "flakes," the thorny rakes, the births of new-born bonny babies or the girth of old, worn, bony ladies with scabies. He scoffed on the kitchen cup-cakes, scuffed on the Halloween capes, roughed on the sweat-dirty neck napes, toughed out the all-wearing out hand brakes, buffed on the ball-bearings in front brakes, huffed on the incredulous *gaffes* from giraffes, sucked-up to the incredible gapes from the Papes, hand-sickled the forlorn *Grapes of Wrath,* thumb-pickled on the well-worn wrath of grapes, rode in a *Taxi Driver* by one Travis Bickle but was not a bit tickled by the well-torn scourge of rapes, cussed Nicolai Kruschev for his hammer and sickle (not to mention Kremlin drapes), rewound His tricky-dickie Nixon tapes, rebound fizz trickle-dickle napes, had no time for cheap jesters' jeers or non-alcoholic beers, watched out-takes of His younger-years, repented the mistakes of His yester-years,

138

looked forward to the retirement-home dances of His latter years, traveled far and un-raveled near, would disappear and re-appear, a grinning peregrinate, a P.O.M.E. pomegranate, a phallic polysyllabic, a polyphonic symphony, a polymorphic polyhedron, a polyglot polygamist, a polychromous polonaise, a poltroonic poltergeist, a polygonal polygynyst, a polynomial Polynesian, a polytechnic polytheist, He studied with a Seer, never had fear, took to learning Shakespeare-speak with King O'Leary Lear, became amusable and confusable, diffusible and excusable, fusible and inexcusable, infusible and losable, trans-fusible and usable, and even with time on His hands stopped watching His watch-piece, adjusted his clock-piece, stopped poking the mantelpiece, left dear Deirdre in reverie, let Delia sail away to Delagoa Bay, left della Robbia working terra cotta, He timely gave up his mistress-piece, made un-timely mattress-peace with Nora, went *deux chevaux* (her *chapeau*, His *chateau*), became homely and made homilies, made peace with Himself and then and then *only* then, with His *bon-femmie* lady the *bon-hommie* man fought a Hercule war with Poirot, a Herculean battle with Thoreau, and from other lands and overseas, plagued with illness and disease, fatigued with anxiety and un-ease, ruefully scrawling with His well-born hands and cruelly crawling on His well-shorn knees, filled His well-worn pen with ink-well sleaze, sniffed the breeze, ate some cheese, and then through Summer wheeze and Winter-chill freeze, lived His "never, ever" master-peace, fibbed, bibbed, glibbed, ad-libbed, nibbed, quibbed, did His "clever, very" masterpiece, the "one and only" *Ulysses* for all to see, and all of this accomplished without even a grant from Ulysses S. Grant. *Gedanken experiment.*

Fame and Fortune (e.mail from a He.Male).

And in one rueful and clue-full, mute-full and due-full, blue-full and glue-full, hue-full and cue-full, pew-full and queue-full, Sue-full and too full, woo-full and woeful, Yule-full and Zoo-full moment of self-imposed clarity, self-serving hilarity, self-practiced vulgarity, un-even parity, unilaterally declared unadulterated, un-expurgated, excessively eager, earnestly earthen, eccentrically ebullient, echoing ecclesiasticism, eclectic ecstasy, clear acclamation, ecliptic eclogue, ecumenical edibility, edifying editing, educated effervescence, educible efficacy, efflorescent effigy, effronterically efflux, elegantly eglantine, egregious elaboration, elated electrostatics, elegant eleemosynary, elevated elegy, elliptical elocution, elucidative eloquence, emboldened emancipation, embarrassing embellishment, emblazoned embroidery, emblematic embracing, emerald embroidery, emerging emeritus, emersion emigration, eminent emolument, emotional empathy, empirical emphasis, empowered employment, empyreal emulation, encephalic enchantment, enclitic enchase, encompassing enclave, encyclopedic endearment, endemic endeavor, enduring endogamy, enervating enfilade, enforcing engagement, engrossing enigma, enjambment enjoyment, enlightening enounce, enraptured enrichment, ensconce ensemble, enshrouded enshrinement, ensuing enterprise, enthralling enthusiasm, enticing entomology, entrancing entourage, enveloping enunciation, enviable environ, envious epexagesis, epic ephemerae, epidemic epicene, episodic episcopacy, epithetic epithalamium, epochal epitome, equitable equerry, errant ermine, esculent escritoire, Esculapian escutcheon, especial esoteric, espousal *esprit*, essential essay, esurient ethics, Etonian etiquette, Eucharistic etymology, Euclidean eudemonism, euphoric eulogy, euphonic euphemism, evolving euphoria, evangelical euphony, even euphuism, eurhythmic evanescence, everlasting evasion, evolving evolution, explicative exaltation, excogitative exculpation, executive execration, exemplary exegesis, exhilarating exigence, exonerated exile, exoteric exordium, expatriate exorcism, expiated expertism, expostulated expurgator, extinguishable exuvial, extravagant and eerie-eyrie literary violence upon the World's citizenry. *Homo et humanitatis expers et vitae communis ignarus.*

Joyce and Shaw : Literary Giants Together.

The *Scholastic Irishman* (the optimistic pessimist) and Great Britain's *Shavian* (the pessimistic optimist) weaved innovative literary talent, revolutionary novelistic style, confusing explicitness, excruciatingly exquisite interior monologues, complex irreverent references, obscenic genius, portmanteau words, Portmadogic nerds, comedic lyricism and lyric comedy (in the case of the former); and dramatic proliferation, prolific drama, swayed the critics, criticized the essayists, a clear pamphleteer of social reformation, a confused chronicleer of reformed socialism, spewed forth opinionated pubic ramblings, brewed fifth onionated public rumblings, impersonated a rustic impersonal *persona*, detonated a busty personal Ramona, combined an eccentric alter ego with a concentric altar to go, had banned plays, read played bans, was popular with scholars, traveled the World in his Darth-Raider jodpurs, sanctimoniously sunk and Thelonious Monk, actuarially drunk and Judas Priest, celestially self-guided by fart-radar dopplers, and was always a fan of the famed Tottenham Hotspurs, which made Him very decidedly unpopular and deciduously poplar. *Nimiast miseria nimis pulchrumesse hominem !*

The Scholastic Irishman (the optimistic pessimist).

Now Joyce (the Former-Night Sinner) did very mundane things
and not many sane things like opening insane wings in Thailand's
asylums, made a blunt point of not being appointed to bored
Hospital Boards where conviction without fiction, restriction
without diction, restraint without astriction, attrition without non-
fiction made one faint at an attaint, where retorts were thwarted,
rare literary role models were made from Victorian convicts who
"rolled" cigarettes and "trolled" fashion models, where non-
victorious convicts were jailed for their afflictions to non-sexual
predilections, served time for their sexual convictions, were
put in solitary to play solitaire for assault with a battery, where
assignation, resignation, assassination, assiguation, asseveration,
assimilation, assertion and desertion turned well-meaning
librarians into Winter Summerians, and paroled all the prisoners
into the City-full hovels-without-novels and the Bodleian book-
bare barren brothels. His Occidental poetry never accidental, His
Oriental writing ever exciting, the English tomato-writers (with
Sire in the Great) had no time for the Irish potato-blighters (with
fire in the grate), so *He* had no time for "The Times," guarded
His words from "The Guardian," made the "News International"
when He wasn't very fashionable even though the New York
Post first baited Him, feted Him, dated Him, placated Him; then
gated Him, hated Him, late-d Him, tried to mate Him with ugly

Cate instead of trying to date Him with "Kiss-Me-Kate;" never equated Him, never rated Him, never sated Him, never Tate-d Him, never even sent a waiter to wait on Him; and then *finally* and *four-never,* five-ever, fated Him. Scribbling all bloody nighty the Blighter most quietly in His all-hooded nightie in almighty Blighty, He out-wrote all the illiterate newspaper writers, that exclusive *clique* of inclusive blighters, those Devils who can only wrong-print but *His* angels write right, though His writings were too slow for "The Express," His words un-observed in "The Observer," were chain-mailed to the rail at the front of "The Mail," were not even reflected in "The Mirror," never made news-in-the-mews in the weird "News of the World" nor paid his dues-to-the-Jews in the feared "Screws of the World," and had his "Red Devils" Man U scripts at night put to bed in "The Sun" where they never-ever saw the light of day. *Gura mile maith agaibh.*

Great Britain's Shaw (the pessimistic optimist).

Shaw (the Latter-Day Saint) took the language of his countrymen's oppressors, shook the wordly kaleidoscope, book up the worldly biblioscope, disconnected the literary autoscope, peered through the biblical bioscope, X-rayed some daughter's brains cranioscope, water mains seweroscope, open drains down periscope, found no fetid fetal feces with his American colonoscope nor no tepid foetal faeces with his British Ceylonoscope, never fingered his dactyloscope, always illuminated his fluoroscope, went catastrophic with his gastroscope, was terrified by his horoscope, was speared by the sphere of his meteorscope, was magnified by his microscope, was minimized by his macroscope, got an eyeful through his ophthalmoscope, spied on cuckoos with his ornithoscope, cockatoos with his didgeridoodoscope, kangaroos with his Aussiescope, was proctored by a doctor with an imperforate proctoscope, viewed Messina through his retinoscope, went-a-sneezing through his rhinoscope, went-a-reading Sigmund Freud through his sigmoidoscope, boom-boxed mono-aural tones through his stereoscope, showered in his bathyscope, bathed in his bowerscope, diagnosed Seth with his stethoscope, viewed the planet Mars through a Uranoscope, cooed Janet Marrs through the keyholescope, booed jolly jack tars through his telescope, hinted whirring loins on his European uroscope in Canada's Newfoundland while simultaneously, quite extraneously, minted stirring coins in his Utopian Euroscope in his British new found land. *Animus audax, subdolus, varius.*

Malthusian Mal Mots.

He felt Mr. *Wright* was *right* to attend a funeral *rite*; fishermen fish *bass* in ponds, singers sing *bass* in songs, philosophers seek the *base* of all wrongs; the librarian a reference will *cite*, the

145

surveyor will *sight* on the construction *site*; it's a *feat* for the *feet*, eat a *sweet* in a *suite* that has *sweet* violets, is it *fair* at the *Fair* for a *tenor* to sing for a *tenner*, who has the phenomenal *sense* to only spend plenary *cents* on overly expensive pheromal *scents*, and was Joan of Arc *in sense* with *incense* before being *incensed* at being burnt at the stake (a well-done *steak* or a *sear* of a *Seer*). Eric *Idle* (when busy) was an *idol*, Tommy *Steele* would *steal steel* without missing a trifle, Adam Faith was unfaithful, Marianne Faithful was dressed-down and stressed-out with pencil-legged Mick, a mediaphile to the masses, lay down with the upper-classes, was stuck-up to the lower classes, and never read music without a really good pair of glasses. The London Symphony will siphon your money under the great Bell of *Bow*, the cellists will *bow* to be *heard* by the *herd* and then *bow* to the audience; the fairy-bound Santa Claus says bone-head "*Ho, Ho, Ho,*" the prairie-bound want a clause that homesteads "*hoe, hoe, hoe,*" He figured out how farmers *produce* their *produce*, they *bolt* the door before the colt makes a *bolt* for it, you can't legally *flog* a horse but you can illegally *flog* cans of dog-meat, and at the horse-racing *Track* you *track* the racing horses before you *fix* the stirrups to *fix* the race, secure the saddle with a *buckle* so the mare doesn't *buckle* under the *weight*, especially if there's a *wait*, making sure to get the jockey to *fast*, and bind him *fast* to the *reins* for

146

a *fast* start when it *rains*. Hospitals have patience for patients, and He triggered-out how the *Nurse* had to *nurse* a Dallas Burn, having already *wound* the bandage around a *wound*, all doctors were *qualified* but not all *qualified* successes, some are *critical* to students but that's not always *critical,* nurses are *patient* with a critical *patients*, usually it's the *custom* for Cardiac Consultants to wear *custom*-made jackets; not all judges wear *law suits* for *lawsuits*, cirrus harvesters have a *hay day* whilst circus car-jesters have a *heyday*, you *hire* lumberjacks to cut *higher* trees, garbage-men *refuse* some *refuse* where artists *mold* vamp siblings and damp buildings grow *mould*, how maids *polish* the *Polish* furniture, took the *lead* as they *led* roof-workers to *lead*, you knead mead for cooks but who will *read* a ton of *red* books which after are *read*, infra-*red* cameras see how foreign *legions* with *lesions* sometimes *desert* in the *desert* after *dessert,* a *waiter* will *wait her* at the *table*, will *table* her the menu (shouldn't a menu for a woman be a *womanu* ?) he will *garnish* her saladry just right or they will *garnish* his salary alright, as it's at His *place* to *place plaice* on the plate that is laid in her *place* at his table. A *deer* is *dear*, a *boar* can be a *bore* but so can a drill, au un-interesting *board* makes you feel *bored*, *beans* have *been* cooked as has-*beans*, refried by has-*been's*, and it's with *disgust* that *this gust* is caused by being beaten by your *staff* in Staffordshire *(Staffs)* with *staffs* (or *staves*) which *stave*-off *staffs* in Staffs but not the house-staff in hospitals who *house house-staph staph*. There is no time like the *present* to *present* a *present*, when shot at the *dove* immediately *dove* into the bushes, who'd have a *swallow* of an oven-baked *swallow*, is it *farther* to *Father* in old Preston Hollow, the lovers don't *object* to the *object* of *their* affections *there*, an *invalid* can have *invalid* insurance, the oarsmen had a *row* over how to *row* in the boat, the door-man was too *close* to Glenn *Close* to *close* the door on her coat, you can't *box* in a *box*, the boxing *rings* can't start until the opening-bell *rings*, the *dear deer* male *buck* will *buck*, the dear deer female *doe's* often *does* what-the-fuck, playing *rugby* in *Rugby* there's always a ruck, a *duck* asunder will always *duck* under a Galway-bound truck, mid-summer's *Puck* plays hockey with a goal-scoring *puck*, you can *tuck* Friar *Tuck* warmly *in* at the *Inn*, a seamstress *sewer* can fall in the *sewer*, but a farmer's *sow* can't learn to *sow* truffels. "*Sew* what" (said the sewing machine as it balked in the nudist camp), "*so* what" said the brewing latrine as it talked in the Buddhist damp), the sinner makes *amends* while the priest *amends* the amen, if there's a culprit in the pulpit it can *alter* the *altar*, don't be *incensed* by the *incense* in the Cathedral at *Coyne* but in the collection plate place a *coin*, a sort of a borrowing *lent* in *Lent*. Captain *Pugh* went *phew !* at the smell of his sailors in the wood-chopped *pew*, they would then *wind* winches to the *wind* and then *bale* like mad, the magistrates bind wenches to the mopped-wood in the jails of the sinned, and then *bail* them very glad; the jailer got a *pail* from *beyond the Pale* and while Norman Mailer goes *pale* in cold Lanarkshire, the tailors sew *sails* from the *sales* and then *sail* in *Sale*, Lancashire. Now the soggy Scottish highland laddies and *lassies* with their boggy English lowland doggies called *Lassies,* the ladies in bin-rows and widows in windows, the tear-jerkers in weirs and the weird-workers from Sears, all mess whatever, press whenever, address whoever, stress *wherever* at a *wear-ever* address on what to *wear* at *Ware.* He was *aware* to be *wary* of not driving when *weary*, delivered *stationary* in *stationary* traffic, when the *fowl* tasted *foul* He *complemented* His dinner with wine *complimentary*, would *accept* a gift *except* when was rude or very rudimentary, was *intolerant* of *intolerable* people, when swimming He *foundered*, when fishing for *flounder* He *floundered*; when mountain-climbing He would *peek* at any *peak* that would *pique* His interest, hated the rain to *pour* on *poor* people, hated *guerrillas* who shot *gorillas* even when there was an *ordinance* against *ordnance*, helped the police *elicit* information about *illicit* activities, but never figured out how the *Strait* of Hormuz wasn't *straight*, even though George *Strait* did. He ate four-*course* dinners with publiners, berate five *coarse* sinners in the law-courts Dubliners, watched

Pasteur put out to *pasture*, built an oil *derrick* with soiled *Derek*, wore His *panama* hat with *Panama* Jack, witnessed the Grim *Reaper* and a pram *raper*, spent the *morning* in *mourning* and then sprained His *lumbar* spine lifting *lumber*. School *Principals* work tirelessly to teach drool *principles*, dentists make your teeth *number* after a *number* of injections, *whether* you *weather* the *weather* depends on infections, Father *Neal* will *kneel* after umpteen genuflections, at communion a *tear* in your stocking-thigh brings a *tear* to the mocking eye, and the *Judge* will *judge* sex-offenders and *subject* the *subject* to cross-examination for being *intimate* with an *intimate* friend, like *perverts extraordinaire* who always butt-her with butter. Doggies *do* do-do in the wet morning *dew*, which is instant relief to the vet-scorning, sweat-pouring, early-morning *you*. TV makes you merry with Mayberry's May Berry, an arboretum *pines* for their *pines*, a tow-truck *tows* and fights gas-saving vandals, Friar Tuck's *toes* and lights Mass-praying candles; especially for dead-beats with skipped heart-beats who have pain *terminal* in a train *Terminal*, after sunrise it's easy to have *missed* the *mist*, you can *rue* a kissed moment in *la rue*, tiny Tina with *huge Hugh* must hustle when *bussed* on her *bust*, and a lady must *bustle* to keep up her *bustle*. In Asia Minor the *minors* grow rice and the *miners* mine mines, in Asia

Major the Chinese *Major* will *major* in English (without a trailer-hitch) with ex-Prime Minister John Majors (who grows sailor-rich), gets his suits off Mr. *Taylor* the *tailor*. In the Republic of Ireland *Pete* digs up the *peat*, in Northern Ireland you buy box-lunching *meat* at the fox-hunting *Meet*, in the short knight's way in a long night's day where the *sloe* of the blackthorn grows *slow*, you can contemplate *Dawn* at *dawn*, *march* April in January and *March*, you *may* or *may not* inseminate *May* in February, June is *due* in July, is *Jew* in September, and while Augustus Caesar was *auguste* in *August* we never found out who *stayed* with *staid* Eve on the "Eve of All Hallows." (But the record will show, the moon's all aglow, astray in the snow, her feet in defeat, ne'er a seat in the sleet but with err in the sheet, she was saved from the gallows, her cheeks very sallow, her muddy feet wallow, her fields hardly fallow, her parents from Mallow, she escaped doom and gloom, they lowered the boom, and her conceived womb when she wed two weeks later was frozen and repugnant, Jovian and abearant, *hosen* and aberrant, Posen and forebearant, chosen and sextant, foreverly forechosen seven months pregnant, but ended up post-magnanimously in a manner most abortifacient). *Praedictum tibi ne nagare possis, si fur veneris, inpudicus exis.*

The Grammatical Anagramatic Grammarian.

He granted that a Presbyterian was *best in prayer*, an Astronomer
was a *moon starer*, The Eyes *they see*, His Dormitory a *dirty
room*, hated Snooze Alarms *alas no more z's,* used The Morse
Code so that *here comes dots*, knew full well that A Decimal
Point fixed Him as *I'm a dot in place*, played Slot Machines
which left Him with *cash lost in me*, called Election Results *lies,
lets recount*; fully realized that Animosity *is no amity*, he proved
that Eleven Plus Two equalled *twelve plus one,* recognized
The Earthquakes as *that queer shake*, and was Germanized to
realize that his Mother-In-Law was a *woman Hitler*. N'er one
for frustration, though upset with His Nation, defied British
subjugation, reviled forced castration, feared eternal damnation,
sought lietrary exonneration, never failed to meet wife Nora at
the station, He never murdered a word with ablation, and was
filled with elation when in Desperation *a rope ends it*.

International Travels.

The *aroma* in *Roma* is simply delightful, a coma in Tacoma is
quite seemingly frightful, Snow White gets finger-tip colder
and vinegar-sip *bolder* when bowling a snow-covered *boulder*
in Colorado Boulder. Was very *bold* as a cricket-slip bowler
and would *bowl* over a Snow Man with a disjointed shoulder,
put down His cigarette holder, and ate out of his supper-time

bowl as the evening grew colder. Now Jim Crow with Crow Indians was always unlucky, Jack Daniels drank Old Crow in crow-covered Kentucky, in old Bowling Green there are newer bowling greens where you can get a hot shower but never the "cold shoulder." In Australia there was plenty to do with a didgeridoo or serenade the old north whales in the New South Wales gales.In American Samoa they know the intents of the New Testament (talofalava), in British Samoa they flow into the new tents of the Old Testament (taro and lava), they have new zeal in New Zealand and found new veal in Newfoundland, there's new found graffiti in Tahiti, old Clint on the dole in Chelsea told Clinton Chelsea on a roll that "New Age" tensioners have become Old Age Pensioners, and now old York of England (with vague Edmund of Langley dead in his grave) and old Amsterdam of Holland (they were suave in The Hague) was next New Amsterdam (1613). In *Amerigo's* (1507) Manhattan, it's now old, bold, cold, sold, gold, "to have and to hold" New York (1664) where everyone drinks Manhattan's, winks are forgotten, sinks are begotten, sewers smell rotten, no-one wears cotton, yet lovers besotten; and in New Netherland in *Vespucci's* (1592) New Jersey, freedom was trampled on, the tramps were rankled on, Karl Marx wrote *Das Kapital*, the Johnny Rebs never marched on the capital, and the Jews invested their capital in a *gedankenexperiment* with significant collateral. Danken Got ! Shalom along came the Kibbitzers, with their despicable sisters; brothers Schmuck (in a smock) and Shmock (in the muck); cousins Klutz (with holes in his socks) and Klotz (with a pain in his guts); aunts Mashugga (with the tea) and Meshughe (with the sugar); a misfit Mieskeit, a nerdy Nudnick, a K'vetsh from Kiev, a Shikseh from Sikkim, a Shmendrik spendthrift, a Shmutter (with the patter) a Shmatter (with a putter); a wide-awake Shnorrer, Bubbee the bubba, a Shnoe in the snow, an infected Toches infected with roaches, a Shtik with a stick, a Naches eating nachos, a Celt without Gelt, a Bobkes with a bobcat, a Tsores from the Azores with his legs full of sores, a Shmuts who'd gone nuts, and the complete Loch in kop, came armed with a mop, jumped out of the Shul into the Kibbutz, smeared the Kaddish with raddish, tiered the boy Goy with their Soy dish, poured it all on the gelfilte fish, stained Drek with their dregs, put their clothes on some pegs, ate a consume of eggs, in a commune everyone begs, then they pulled off their shoes and rested their legs. Gai Avek ! "Where you from" asked the Frum, "we're a communion of one" answered a nun, and with a Chutzpah from a cheetah, a Mazel Tov from Judy, a Mitzvah in a Bar, a Mitzveh from a bat, they prayed under a Shaitel, ate their K-kosher trifle, at the Talmud had an eye-full, slept under the sky-full protected by a rifle owned by Harvey Keitel. Now when the Washingtonian Capitals proposed a State Capitol, they were in a state of despair when denied by King George's inapparent heir, the Capital State was in a state of disrepair and when it was finally placed in a residential gorge Washington State, President George Washington had a *statue* of such *stature* that they had to write a *statute* to preserve it. Residential Hoboken was clearly *verboten*, so all the Channel Island's New Jerseyites set their old flannel jerseys alight, then vamped on and bent on, vented and dented on, Wells Fargo'd and sent on, and would always repent on that the British had taken their land without ever paying the rent on, so they all renamed the state of their State Capitol within the capital of Trenton. A Meister and a mister (after the death of his sister), on a wandering, wondering, wending, winding, wanderlust *weltanschauung* met a *wunderkind-mit-welttschmerz* in a *realpolitik leitmotiv*, an utterly introspect *urtext* on a locomotive to Utrecht, the *echt ersatz* first-class was up-market *kaffeeklatsch*, a *gestalt bildungsroman* past Roman buildings, from the Hinterland to the Netherlands, *sprachgefuhl* and peaceful, *spiel* and gleeful, *schmalz* and malts, *angst* and Yanks, *zeitgeist* and Jesus Christ, *kitsch* and stitch, and once again ended up, where else ? But Hoboken ! *Gotterdammerung.*

An Apothecary of an Aristocracy.

Captain John Smith Esquire, My.Vet.Him.Amass.Rice.Corn
from ye olde England claimed, shamed, blamed, gained, lamed,
maimed, pained, tamed, brained, and dame'd twelve East sea-
board estates, divided them up into six least Fee-Lord states,
Squireing and acquiring Me.Vt.NH.Mass.RI.Conn from His
Royal Lowness, the Prince of Whales, KG, KT, OM, GCB, AK,
QSO, PC, ADC, Earl of Chester, Duke of Cornwall, Duke
of Rothesay, Earl of Carrick, Baron of Renfrew, Lord of the
Isles, Prince and Great Steward of Scotland and vowed *tenets*
in *tents* to undercharge *tenants*, got patriot *counsel* to *council*,
consult the *Consul*, was *discreet* which street was such a
discrete entity in which Crete, announced the *imminent* arrival
of the *eminent* President, did *forward* the *foreword*, then
flaunted the faxed facts of Constitutional law to the fascimile
British constitution with great *effect* who arrogantly *flouted*
the old *colonial* law with poor *affect* in the New *Colonies*. It
was the end of delusional *reigns*, the start of diluvial *rains*, the
Monarchy let go of the *reins*, a chilling Churchillian rhetoric,
a *win-some* and lose-some paregoric, a *winsome* congregation
and loose fun conversation of parochial church hill, and at the
Metropole it was announced antimetabole *the beginning of*
the end, it was, perhaps, the end of the old rule of Home Rule
and the start of a new beginning. (The constant British fear

of incontestant Brachylogia received *one blow after another,*
terrible losses, frightful dangers, everything miscarried and
Anaphora *lost on the beaches, on the landing grounds, in the*
fields, in the streets, in the hills, and eventually surrendered).
The oxymoronic morons proclaimed that a *curtain of freedom*
descended across the North American continent and the
moronic, paradoxical Metonymy reclaimed America was
welcomed to her rightful place, her flag welcomed upon the seas
and Thanks-Giving day renamed Litotes *during alterations*
to the map of Europe. Thus re-named *Newe Englande,* where
early clam chowder was made from damn powder, they always
slept warm and bold in their *red socks,* ran hot and cold with
their *Red Sox,* their tan rags tagged under the bed-skirts, they
then ran ragged over the Red-Shirts, they dumped the *damned*
tea in the harbor, clumped the *dammed* sea with their ardor,
had their bear-locks rut, their hair-locks cut, and the Boston
Pops played just a day ago in the cold snow aglow, the *adagio*
of sweet Samuel Barber. The Romans never *conquered* old
Caledonia but the French *conkered* New Caledonia with three
shots of a "one-er," a "two-er" of cognac, a "three-er" in Trier,
but in *Hibernia* and *Pays de Galles* the weather is harsh, the
country is marsh, the thirsts of the workers are incredibly
parched, the shirts of the gentry are brilliantly starched, the
rich people dine, the poor folks eat; the merchants in sandals,

the urchins bare feet; the farmers pick corn, the hobos dig beet; the gardeners pick apples, the combines mow wheat; in winter its cold, in summer the heat; at funerals you say goodbye, at weddings you meet; country girls are blousy but school-marms are neat; *au-paire* girls with a "big *pair*" always appear to eat a *pear sweet;* the industrialists mine coal, the peasants dig peat; the village has a Town Hall, the County a "Seat;" and while nursing mothers distress, cursing others in dress, even the Manor of the Mistress have nursing nipples, the ruminants are set on, their offspring are let on, Oh ! What Divine Intervention as all the new-born calves know how aggressively with great serendipity to mistress the manner to suck on a teat. *Ad Majorem Dei Gloriam.*

The Non-Moronic Oxymoronic.

The Geordies at Wear created Newcastle-on-Tyne *sellers* on top of old castle wine *cellars* (where disease bites you with Lyme), whilst the Georgies in Staffordshire berated Newcastle-Under-Lyme beggars on top of new hassle reggaes (where surcease invites you with wine), yet on long summer days nobody notices the time, the weather turns fine, the visitors toe-the-line, it's "never yours" but it's "mine," its light at five and dark by nine, the woodlands grow cottonwoods and tall-growing pine, the "Deutsche Volk" cruise on and booze on the

Rhine, the Scottish eat haggis and sing Auld Lang Syne, the French are all sipping on the "fruit of the vine," the mummers will very cleverly act out a mime, the visitors observe the locals through ambivalent bifocals, and the pleasantry of the peasantry never notices the trousers of the regenerate yokels help up with degenerative twine. Hut *artists* sketch in Scotland but *artistes* drink Scotch in Ireland, the *drunk* is *drunk* on cheap whisky but won't *drink* sea-water in the "*drink*," they are sick-a-more of Sycamore in wood-paneled forests, there is no egg in eggplant, no ham in a hamburger but *der Berger* in Hamburg hams-it-up for *der ham* in Durham. There's no apple or pine in a ripened pineapple, the *apple-of-his-eye* is a Father's daughter, English muffins are French and french fries are English, sweetmeats aren't sweet but are candies, Candy is dandy while sweetbreads aren't bread but can be consumed with a "dandy," quicksand moves slowly (move if you dare), boxing rings are "squared-circles" (that means a square), guinea-pigs aren't from Guinea nor are *real* pigs (yet still cost a guinea-a-pair), Greenland is ice but Iceland is green, but there's no home in auld Ireland like Tim-n-Tillie's "Derreen." Us USA writers *all write*, that's okay in UK and in Dublin *alright*, but fingers don't *finge*, grocers don't *groce* and hammers don't *hamme*; a rock-n-roll band can *jam* in a traffic-*jam*, it's all bread-and-*jam*; but one tooth is a tooth but two are your teeth, one booth is a booth but not a plural of *beeth*, one goose is a goose and two are the geese, but two moose are two moose and not a rural of *meese*; when school-day is over the school-teachers have *taught,* the little boys *taunt*, the school-flag is *taut*, but when church-day is over you can't say the church-preachers have *praught*, and if a vegetarian eats vegetables, what do humanitarians eat ? And if we are what we eat, why don't we eat people who are better looking and wealthier than we are ? Actors recite at a play, but musicians play at a recital; we can ship cargo by truck and truck cargo by ship, not very insightful; yet our noses run and our feet smell, quite decidedly frightful ! Does a "slim chance" and a "fat chance" have the same odds ? A "wise man" and "wiseguys" are oxymoronic, but that's up to the Gods. Why doesn't car "Buick" rhyme with par "quick," it's a confusing conundrum that's "out for the kick." In small Ireland towns you can be "looking out for the *craig*," but in big dire-land cities you are "looking in for the *crack*" and while the Marquis of Queensbury rules put you "out for the count," the mark of the Queen fools you "in with the Count." Thus a house "burns up" as it burns down, you fill in a form by "filling it out," an alarm "goes off" by going on, the celestial night *stars* are always invisible (even when they're *out* and the house lights are on), the terrestrial film *stars* are always visible (when the fans are *out* and the floodlights are off), deep in the heart of Texas the stars at night are big and bright (when streetlights are on, the seat lights are off, the movie stars are in, the heavenly stars are out) and the ushers *screen* the patrons, while "hushers" scream at matrons before the movie *screen*. But *yet* fresh *bets* are drying, *Yeti* Fliedermaus *bats* are sighing, baseball *bats* are flying, cigarette-*butts* are dying, big-*butts* are crying, grammatical *buts* are sighing, cricket *bats* are buying, doormats are trying and computer *bits* are frying when the bestial-might boxing-Czars *put out the lights* after their boxing heroes *"put out the lights"* of the pretenders and contenders. He wondered why the third hand on a watch was called the second hand, if a word was mis-spelled in the dictionary how would He ever know, and if Webster wrote the first dictionary, where did he find the words ? He wondered why "slow down" and slow up" meant the same thing, or why a "fat chance" and a "slim chance" mean the same thing. He saw "tug" boats push barges, automobiles drive on the parkway yet park on a driveway, while He put his suits in a garment bag He saw Nora put her garments in a suitcase while neither paid charges. Her bra was singular but her panties were plural, and she never wore either while painting a mural. He was sorry for cross-eyed writers with dyslexia, He himself had dyspepsia, but spent all His time writing and dieting that he was blessed with cachexia. Only had one radio so why was it a set ? It was easily heard, and why didn't glue stick to the inside of the bottle like curd, and He came away exasperated that abbreviated was such a long word. And at opening night of "The Glass Menagerie" playwright Williams in Tennessee tasks to ask where was Mickey Mouse when the lights went out? A Tallahassee *Toff he* once answered between mouthfuls of *toffee* that poor little Mickey was "lost in the dark." *Ars longa, vita brevis.*

The Professional Paraprosdokian of Prose.

He always asked God for a bike to enhance His business, and when not forthcoming just stole a bike and asked for forgiveness. Never went to church to become a good christian any more than standing in His garage made Him a car, when a door is not a door its always ajar. Once argued with an idiot but was dragged down to the other's level and incessantly beaten with the other's experience, so agreed with the idiot so both could be wrong to His own deleterience. He was enlightened that light travelled faster than sound, another appeared bright until opening his mouth to expound, thats why a bus always travels twice as fast when you run after it than when you are in it upwound. The early bird gets the worm while the second mouse gets the cheese, dolphins in captivity train people to give them thrice-a-day feeds, knowledge is knowing that a tomato is a fruit and sow are the seeds. *Sui generis.*

The Well-Heeled and Barrow-Wheeled Wordsmith.

From then on He wrote *alcaics* in Aramaic, wrote graphics of *sapphics,* wrote the *pantoum* of the opera, *they* insisted that His manner desist, His banner resist, got His knickers in a knot but not a snickers in His *thesis.* When upset with a quickstep with a stuck-up woman would *double dactyl* a sidestep with a Piltdown Man, and after afternoon tea and before laughter-swoon glee, wrote six terse *ballads* for salads, five verse *ballades* for sad lads, *epics* for four-day trips, three short *tales* for Mr Hoffmann in two long tails, exquisite *romances* for single dances, inquisitive *elegys* for graveyards, shady *pastorals* for Lady Astor's pals, clerical *lyrics* for cynics, *inflated proverbs* in community-gated suburbs, deflated *mnemonics* in segregated cherubs, Don redouble your prose at speaking the impregnable *redouble* and Ron do trust your nose at tweaking the impregnated *rondeau,* thrice-troubled His efforts to mold Smetana's *The Moldau,* first in Moldavia and then in Moldova; gave short-rope to *mope poem* and when had them printed couldn't wait to show 'em, performed *chants royal* for elephants loyal, *kyrielles* instead of Kerie's, *triolets* for violets, *rondels* for blonde belles, *roundels* for scoundrels, *rondelets* for Rhonda Letz, wrote *monometers* through a monocle, *dimeters* in diameter, *trimeters* in a trimester, *tetrameters* with an ammeter, *pentameters* in St Peter's, *hexameters* in a Mexican theater, *heptameters* with hepatitis, *octometers* with optometers, and

dipped into dictionaries for quite distinctive *distichs* for servicing
her Mercedes limousine with oil-free dispticks, or making up
her facial-clean with animal-free lipsticks, for the always scene,
never seen, ever clean, never obscene, Frau Marlene Dietrich
the *decastich*. Once out with Basil, He got on the razzle (with the
Moors on the moors), it turned into a frazzle (with the Persians
chasing in the Permian Basin), then a razzle-dazzle (with amatory
Arabs and bacchanalian Bahrainis), and perfected the use of the
odious *ghazal* (which for the un-initiated is always pronounced
"gazzle"). It's *glosa* in Spain but *the glose* in Gloucester, He used
tribachs for three Bachs, a colossus of *molussus, amphimacers*
for amphitheaters, *baccius* for Bacchus, *antibaccius* for auntie's
"back-up" knees, *ditrochees* for Durocher fees, *paeons* for the
pions, *choriams* for the litle lambs, and was unusually trite when
his appetite for *epitrites* was quite satisfied. *Acatalectic* verse gave
Him atelectasis, bucolic *diaeresis* gave Him colic *and* diuresis, *arsis*
was catharsis, *caesura* gave him seizures, was wham-jambed and
jam-bammed with *enjambement*, *ictus* made infants kernicterus,
made Icarus melt and most of the men unfairly itchy, made sick-
are-us Celt and the women fairly bitchy; massacred a *lai* at My Lai
(that's a *virelai* truth), and both forms are acceptable, both modern
and *ancien* for sister Aleutians and old and *nouveau* for
Mr. Trudeau. He composed *clerihew* in the foggy dew, went berserk
with the diversification of His *versification,* farted *vowels* with His

bowels, He quoted *limericks* from County Limerick about two flute-tooting tutors with two tooth-muting flutes who tutored two tooters to toot on a flute, He spoke *little willies* that enraptured Big Willy's, and He spoke with an accent so that His unaccented *syllables* sounded like silly bills, an ideologue with a monologue, a dinosaurus born in Taurus, a "never-saw-us" born in a *Tourister*, a conversationalist also-ran, a monologist better-than, and just when He saw us, we knew He wanted to Lesseps and stress us, core us and door us, figurine and four us, jaw us and whore us, lore us and more us, ignore and paw us, roar us and tour us, yore us and tore us, your us and store us, gore us and bore us, but when we looked His way, then He ran away, He just kicked up His heels, and then disappeared down the street, and then eventually re-appeared in the library with His thesaurus. *Magister Artium.*

A Rhyme in Time is Eighth.

By now His *elegaic verses* were elegant and when His *verses* weren't fit for vespers, wrote *iambic* verse with a pen enscribed "I am Bic," *trochaic* verse with a trochar, *anapestic* verse with an antiseptic stick, *dactylic* verse with a forefinger, *metric* verse with four fingers, *chain verse* when locked up, His *blank verse* was free, His *free verse* was blank, His *acrostic verse* very agnostic, His *double acrostic* tersely prognostic, *alphabetical verse* very ascetical, His *circular verse* very square-in-the-round, His *daisy-chain*

verse was sold for a pound, His *nonsense verse* made sense to Him
and nobody else, the terse alcoholics never understood
His verse *univocalis*, and He *always* had the last word with a *first-word rhyme* even though nothing is neater than a broken parking
meter than was "Educating Rita" where they *all* got the *rhyme*
wrong. He tried *nursery rhymes rewritten* but the children weren't
smitten, He composed *monorhymes* in Manor times, *triple rhymes*
in crippled times, *double-end rhymes* for triple-beginning dimes,
multirhymes for the McNulty Times, *internal rhymes* for fraternal
wines, *leonine rhymes* for nine leopards, *eye rhymes* for deaf actors,
rime riche for a multitude of factors, paraphrased the *pararhymes*
for parachuting Argentines, fixed *broken rhyme*, charmed
grotesque rhyme, synthesized *synthetic rhyme*, wrote *pruned rhyme*
for prudes, never back-tracked with *back-track rhyming*, spoke
rhymed verse disguised as prose which sounded as timed verse
recognized by pro's, His *correct rhyme* incorrect, His *incorrect
rhyme* correct, and then got the *cast* of The Outcasts to *cast* out the
remains of his legumes and rhymes, thrown overboard by grown
overlords just like rinds in the Rhine. *Angst in der Hinterland.*

The Poet of Prudism.

He boasted assuredly with *assonance*, boated constantly
consonance with Constance, invented *indentation* with
concentration, and never once said "verbode" when mere danger

166

bodes, He would Mazzerati the roads, confuse the *literati* with codes, furnish his *antenati* with loads, introduce the *illuminati* to modes, lost the papparazzi in groves, and let all the toads hop in from Rhodes, *inhabitati* His abode while He spent all His latter years reciting His *odes*. His *couplets* were *Chaucerian* and recited by Dr Kervorkian, were *heroic* and frequented by Stoics, the wife-in-His-life had two sets of *triplets*, one *Tennysonian*, one Ionian, and the other one stayed home in the dome all-alone again. *Cinquains* were nice silly-bill counters for window-sill mounters, His *tenses* made no sense and nonsense and confused the senses, the *englyn* were born in Glynbourne before he learnt tenses, His Japanese *haiku* was sold and Irish U2 was told "take a hike, you," He was stunned by the chimes of the *punned rhymed haiku*, the *naga-uta* was never taught (ah !) in Utah, did Monet hear a *nonet* at tennis ? His *tercets* were terse and imperfect, He always said "hello, *Madam I'm Adam*" when out in the garden, but never wrote my *rhopalics* with his phallus in the metropolis, but did halt a *tanka* with a grenade in Granada, wrote similar tongue-in-cheek *palendromes* when writing Himler plays for the Hippodrome, wrought dissimilar dung-in-beak *malendromes* when scribbling at-home-alone, His "*Quatrain* from Lake Ponchetrain" was eerily inane and really insane, His *quintain* from sunny Spain caused unbearable pain and was equally mundane, His *sestet* from Dorset was embarrassing to sisters in corsets, the *septet* was *rhyme royal*, the *octet* was blind toil, the *ottava rima* was Operatic Diva, cross the *Sicilian octave* and you've got one foot in the grave, the *nine-line stanza* was performed by a choir extravaganza, the *Burns stanza* was turned into a Broadway bonanza, whilst the *Venus and Adonis Stanza* traveled to the Tokyo Ganza, where it became a "B" movie starring Mario Lanza. His *sonnets* were applicable for New York Taxi bonnets, whether *petrarchan* for Farrakan, *spenserian* for Lady Di, *Miltonian* for Keyes, *Shakespearean* for shaking spears again, *succinct* as distinct, and made up a play about Violet the *triolet* who got squashed like a mellon and inadvertently washed down the toilet. *Delicias illepidae.*

The Alphabetic Ambassador.

His *novellas* leaked permanently like worn-out umbrellas, His *sestinas* (both rhymed and unrhymed) were destined for the Central Park latrinas (both grimed and un-grimed), the New York Times that displays "all the news that's fit to print" but "dissed" His plays which were "no news" and "unfit to squint," led forays of "nay-says" to discourage his nightly plays, made His *mot juste* not just, sent *epigrams* by telegram, composed *jingles* in singles, *blues* in the pews, and *calypsos* so "tippy-toed" for California-bound Caliphs. He would de-scribe the writing and describe the writers, took risks with *asterisks,* drove straight through the *Full Stop* signs, found out that (American) female writers wrote *period* even when not on a "period," an astronomical anatomical who became very comical when dealing with *commas,* became very ironical when the good Doctor told Him he had a *hemi*-colon instead of a *semi*-colon, wrote hymns made out of *homonyms,* wrote *phoneme's* but phoned *you,* never de-hyphenated a virgin, wrote respectfully about women with *hyphens,* greeted simple Simon the pie-man as a "pie-in-the-sky" man, a nobody knows "why ? man," he saluted Jacob Wyman and Aaron Whyman, acknowledged Isaac Hymann with "Hi, Man," and then defenestrated Lady Queensberry with a touch to the hymen. He eclipsed his *ellipsis,* made catastrophe's out of *apostrophe's,* would take a "slash" in the wood when writing a *slash,* would *predicate* a pharmacist, read so fast his 100-word sentences were like 100-yard *dashes,* wrote an *Em dash* for hesitators, penned an *En dash* for pontificators, quote *Ogden Nash couplets* for bolderdash triplets, was Ruth-less after He wrote her a *ruthless rhyme,* wrote *Vers De Societe* for the Sirs of society, made a racket with *brackets,* made notes out of *quotes,* made junctions out of *conjunctions,* never asked his parents where to put the *parentheses,* asked questions at *exclamation marks,* exclaimed at *question marks,* paid penalties for His *penults,* pre-paid His *antepenults,* ate peanuts with Lucy, the biblical Cain found mid-life Doris was past her knack, the diabolical rain drowned Boris Pasternak in his anarak, "there's nothing to worry about" said the optimist, "I worry about that" said the pessimist, life is lived forwards not backwards, but sweet-sleep horizontal. And John Stanley Sweetman was an honorably kind sweet man but I can't place his *alphabet poem* "A Poetic Alphabet" above the Great man's alpha-betting abecedarian. So that's it, *albeit.*

The Prince of Perseverance.

But not to be rude (I hope I'm not boring you), not to be crude (I hope I'm not boar-ing you), hot to be Ruud (I hope I'm not goring you), no woman a dude (I hope I'm not whoring you), not time for food (I hope I'm not gnawing you), when questions are asked "who'd" (I hope I'm not ignoring you), by God it's Saint Jude (I hope I'm not jawing you), I'm not in the mood (for sexually pawing you), when you're in the nude (I hope you're not "I'm-in-you"), who solved the mystery of our dear Edwin Drood (I hope I'm not clawing you), but there is a weird tale told well-worthy of even Edgar Allan Poet himself. When *our* immortal Adonis, so God-like to us we address Him as "He," while writing literary prose or poetic literature (which is it, what do you think, why am I asking *you* ?) in the minature, had mere-mortal moments of human experience as when hen-catching and then watching creep Stirling McMurtle kiss neat Myrtle McWhirtle as she crept in a circle, into the Crypt, to take a quiet crap in the scratching crepe myrtle. (This is clearly insane) ! He was madly incensed with the pain, sadly drenched in the rain, badly benched on *The Maine*, radically quenched in the main, entrenched on the train, but didn't miss whirling Miss Whirtle Mc Myrtle cleanly sighting and diligently wiping her marble-clear, pear-shaped "tush" in the harbor-beer, dare-nape back of a creosote bush. He picked up his crescent wrench, ran after the indecent wench, and caused an almighty stench with His visible *villanelles* which were latterly vilified by the queer Gaston villains, tatterly liquified by the near Aston Villans, matterly satirized by the bedeviled literary ogres, quarterly criticized by the critique-soiled gargoyles of the College of Triest, and always were imitated (but never impersonated) by the burgeoning bourgeons of burlesque at the University Villanova. *Adonis noster,* James Joyce.

The Supersonic Electronic.

He went "trick-cycling" with a Psychiatrist, tilled geoponic with a Slavonic, enjoyed demonic hedonics with a suitor Teutonic, read for a Miltonic, enjoyed delusions of grandeur with a megalomanic Tychonic, wrote numerous mnemonics Ionic, marbled stone-cold floors only onyx, warbled tone-deaf messages telephonic, sprayed plagued-mice bubonic, uttered professional phrases Byronic, played the xylophone un-harmonic, caught bronchitis pneumonic and escaped pneumonia pulmonic, fought wars Napoleonic, sought dinosaurs paleolithic, wrote verses paeonic, prayed to Gods pantheonic, gave charity Free-Masonic, sought myths theogonic, ran races Olympionic, climbed pyramids Pharaonic, wrote music philharmonic, had faults tectonic, thought thoughts synchronic, diagnosed ultrasonic, studied verses Platonic, viewed planets Plutonic, invented circuits micro-electronic, amplified microphonic, sipped clean waters Babylonic, listened to Muddy Waters hydroponic, danced rock-and-roll saxophonic, had relationships platonic, attended Temple Masonic, sailed islands Japonic, held conversations jargonic, changed His appearance chameleonic, wired a robot bionic, spoke articulately and speculatively to a listening aphonic, played music transonic, used hair-thickening tonic, exploded bombs nucleonic, flew jets super-sonic, space capsules stratonic, ate Italian lunches macaronic, weathered hurricanes typhonic, typhoons cyclonic, saved plants and animals zoonic, sent subsonic polyphonics, had bowel movements colophonic, gave birth embryonic, utilized synapses ganglionic, administered saline hypertonic, exercised muscles hypotonic, absorbed sound quadraphonic, mumbled words glottoglonic, then would put out the light, kiss His good wife, and spent the rest of the night with a good gin and tonic. *Wir Danken Got !*

***Exile to Zurich via Ye Olde England (N'er to Sea
Erin's Shore For Never More).***

With His last penny spent, He then traveled with Randall the
vandal to candle-lit Ghent, hobbled in sandals most incredibly
dent, handled a shillelagh most certainly bent, and from behind
a curtain un-certain began rhyming inadvertent, then one
Dublin Advent with His gait circumvolvent, He made His way
circumlocution from His lodgings circumvent and suspect, His
Irish *brogue* circumflex and circumspect, the Heavenly stars
circumpolar rotating, the Hollywood stars circumvallating, with
His pleading "Sir, *cum* for real" girlfriends and His bleeding
circumboreal enemies, never let His apartment insistence
or His personal persistence be dulled by the interminable
and indeterminable, pouring-rain consistent; enlightened Sir
Cumference, a Knight of the Round Table; telegraphed "The
Evening Telegraph" circumvolution with much elocution (hello !
hello ! anybody there ?) with a new manuscript craft but *we*
all know there would be "nothing doing" with their usual,
old man writing craft (well before the unusual, young women
fighting graft), this whole thing is daft, take a shower in Bath,
have a bath in London Tower, even uneven Stephen Dedalus
thought it was perilously garrulous, Hemingway taciturn, at
first out of the fire and into the frying pan, but ended up out
of the Linehan and into the byre. He never enjoyed reserved

meetings with overflow seating, and was always displeased when appointed to totally deserved seating yet always took kindly to any ill-mannered greeting; traveling forever a true treble rebel on the *Aer Lingus* ferry that started from Derry flying the tri-colored white, orange and green, ever-always intended as a rebuke to the Queen, rose up with the "Falling Angels" and sat down with the "Rising Fenians," had tea and cake with the few multi-linguistic Anglo-Irish clinicians and coffee and doughnuts with the most distinguished American physicians, nobly above the couth-less and drinking Nobles on the right and the tooth-less and winking Nobby Stiles on the left of the first-place feted, *summa cum laude* treated, history repeated, in death old, bold and cold, in Heaven pure gold, to have or to hold, far from the earthly pedestal mold to the most prominent fold on the celestial cushions gold, with all His re-written writings, well bode and re-sold to the next highest bidder. *Cui bono ?*

Yearning for Yeats.

He was very much entitled to talk much-a-lot (without having anything to say), sang songs in Camelot (cheerful and gay), served His country in Vietnam a lot (without His friend Ray), liked dating Pam a lot (without leading her astray), always liked to pray a lot (with a flowered bouquet), liked "making hay" a lot (without spiritual decay), kept farm animals in the hayloft (but never a stray), smoked cigarette reefers a lot (without an ashtray), liked cooking lamb a lot (without cooking spray), liked spreading jam a lot (but in His own way), visited the Hoover Dam a lot (but only on holiday), liked eating ham a lot (without having to pay), liked digging up land plots (in flowery May), bespoke languages polyglot (very *touche),* liked flying *Aeroflot* (very *riske),* rounded up scoundrels all around the square, got them to declare the square was really round, the round table really square, whether or not Sir Lancelot was *actually* there to title the manuscript delightfully nice and exquisitely precise, it's forever title, the literary insightful, now very in site-full, the eclectic most spite-full, the invariably delightful, professionally posed, majestically prose, His manuscript titled, "Good, Very." Rutting on a ledge, the sun on the beach, the son of a Beach (Sylvia) re-Joyced, the son-of-a-bitch Editor (Ruttledge) laughed, very ironic, *tres* laconic, "I guarantee this will *not* sell" says he, thereby condemning the Freeman Press and *The Nightly Telegraph* to the (US) garbage can and the (UK) dustbin of history. Much rather than Dan Rather report this *commedie d'errors* on the CBS Evening News, no better Dan than Miss Justice of Carriage to carry *this* miscarriage of justice to the IRA seething pews; wouldn't Yeats's Dan Rather rather "run o'er windy gap" where they could "throw a penny in his cap," Rather Dan "a liveried porter raise his lettered cap." A set of tattered rags upon a stick is good enough for me. *Tempus Fugit.*

Travels in the Twentieth Century.

The Turner Network Television commanded a TNT inquisition, The Nightly Telegraph recommended a TNT deposition, their all-bitter staff drank their brown-and-mild draft then cut *The Joyce Draft* in half, they put the editorial and primordial knife to the "Fatted Calf," the end of an old Irish write, the beginning of a new Celtic rite, from an old Brittania-wrong to a new Hibernia-right, so after the Egyptian Pyramids, the hanging Gardens of Babylon, the Mausoleum at Halicarnassus, the Temple of Artemis at Ephesus, the Colussus of Rhodes, the Statue of Zeus by Phidias at Olympia, and the Pharos at Alexandria, Joyce became the Eighth Wonder of the World; and after the Seven Years' War (1756-63) in which England and Prussia defeated Austria, France, Russia, Sweden and Saxony; then waged a twelve years' war (1904-16) in which *Stephen Hero* was defeated and *A Portrait of the Artist as a Young Man* was published. So at the beginning of the day there's not much to say and at the end of the night even more literary gripe. It's a new day's dawn, the lovers fawn, watch Goldie Hawn, mow the linden lawn, the bereaved mourn, the thief pawns, requiem at

Jimmy Vaughan's, Ireland's Shaw with Dallas's Rick Shaw in a rickshaw (note the GB decal) warns "if you let a woman in your life you will have eternal strife." Marriage is like a bird-*Cage aux Folles* where all the ones on the inside are trying to get out and all the ones on the outside are trying to get in, marriage is only for married people, a carriage is cheaper and lasts longer, a garage is sweeter and lasts forever, marriage is not for single people, yet the man always starts the relationship by chasing the woman, and the woman always ends the courtship by catching him. From pillar to post, from the least to the most, from the plains to the coast, from crumpets to toast, from groaning to boast, from Silas Marley the ghost, from visitor to host, from cooking a roast, it's not only basket-ball players who travel "coast to coast." This weary old globe has Anglophobes that disrobe, Francophobes who unrobe, Germanophobes who disrobe, Russophobes who conglobe, Japonphobes with their strobes, Negrophobes in their robes, Sinophobes with SARS microbes, don't miss Miss Loeb with pierced ear-lobes, read the new Book of young Job in tattered old clothes, and we all look away as the homophobes probe. What if gravity *forces* the apple to the ground, shouldn't I get the credit? After all, Sir Isaac Newton got the credit for postulating the apple was "attracted" to the ground, even though apples were "falling" on sleeping heads for at least 25 million years prior to his "observation" ? The limits of our Universe can be approached but not exceeded, that's what stymied Albert Einstein's *Unified Field Theorem,* as the center of our Universe is everywhere but the circumference is nowhere, the center of gravity of the Universe being *outside* the Earth, with the Earth's center of gravity within it. Charles Darwin's theory of Evolution applied to the Galapagos animals he observed, but then became a Seer of Revolution supplied by the Gallipoli pro's, for humans play cellos, invent computers and build airplanes, you never get a thrilla-of-a-kiss from a gorilla-in-the-mist, orangutans are also-rans, the blind organ-grinders monkey is funky, and eating carrots is excellent for eyesight (who has ever seen a rabbit with spectacles) ? James Joyce never said it, I never read it, I ever believe it and that forever settles it. Those were simpler days, them, of Robert Louis Stephenson re-telling piratical tales, Christopher Columbus land-wondering with a map, Ponce de Leon sea-wandering with a sextant, Ferdinand Magellan alas! without a compass and Hernando de Soto ceaselessly adrift with a graph. *Post-hoc propter-hoc.*

The Posthumous Retirement of A Post-Humorous Recluse.

So no time to rejoice with our own Mr re-Joyce, all-pervasive when invisible, all-persuasive when visible, an autocracy in a democracy, the stock of the aristocracy, never a despotocracy of hypocrisy but always a monocracy of nomocracy, from writing slavocracy to publishing snobocracy, a theocracy in the stratocracy, left the mobocracy for the neocracy, hated the hagiography, rebuked the demonocracy, admired the gerontocracy, had no use for the gynecocracy, rose up in the hierocracy, dropped idiocracy for plutocracy, redesigned His logocracy, sped up His pedantocracy, opened a store shopocracy, dug gardens plantocracy, heard words ochlocracy, was an auxiliary for the non-military, a non-auxiliary for the military, and with a declaration of authoration and authentation, He left the large dyslectic disparagings of the inarticulate majority and went out to small eclectic gatherings of the articulate minority, defied conscription and restriction, got up off the Parliamentary side of His *arse,* the parsimonious side of His class, the alimentary side of His *jejunum*, the well side of His *ileum,* the blind side of his *caecum,* the elementary side of His school, standing off-side the two sides of His three-legged stool, or sitting on the seat o'er His peat-smelling stools, so after closing His bowels, He got rid of his trowels, convinced poor Christina to wash all His towels, declined football fouls, scared off His ghouls, quieted His howls, put a set in His jowls, got out His vowels and made a prediction that He would write an hieroglyphic prescription of such exclusively nondescript fiction or of much reclusively manuscript non-fiction and with utmost exclusively ascription would unalterably be most unhappy to have pre-nappy strife, live a post-happy life both ante-humorously, posthumously, a non-public description of pubic non-description, with writing not diction, of fiction without friction, preferring to drive everyone crazy, except when driving Miss Daisy, would make an eternal present of being ever-present on the most pleasant low highway, most peasant high sow-way, most pheasant-fly roadway of sardonic literature, a quaint Irish immature caricature of impeccable character, second-place seated on the silver cushions pleated 'neath the Rock and the Dome of the Heavenly throne, a multitude of one, a coalition of two, a *trifecta* of glee, His reputation to the 'fore, a "high-five" on the side, a six-pack to drink, a seventh Heaven to appreci-eight, nine lives for the cat, ten biscuits for the dog, a sole sincere soul in the physician-position, now filled with contrition, received great admonition and was non-Priestly caste and J. B. Priestly cast, and was forever refined and confined by the Act of Contrition. *Hodie in curia. Nugator !*

Writing Novels in Hovels.

He enjoyed un-reserved meetings with half-empty seating, and was always very pleased when appointed to any non-deserved seating yet always took un-kindly to any well-mannered greeting; He deservedly wrote under-written novels in over-traveled hovels or stayed in under-traveled hovels and wrote over-written novels; wrote fictional illiterate literary passages in over-booked hotels with International travelers without articulate messages or stayed in under-booked hotels without International travelers with inarticulate messages where He wrote non-fictional very literate non-literary passages; wrote under-worded fictional novels with non-literary passages on over-booked steamship passages without intellectual passengers, and traveled on under-booked steamship passages with intellectual passengers and wrote over-worded non-fictional novels with literary passages; and on under-written travels was free to write over-written, fictional novels without literate non-literary passages in over-traveled hovels with architectural passages or in hotels without intellectual passengers with inarticulate messages or on under-booked steamship passages with International travelers, or write under-written non-fictional novels with illiterate literary passages in under-traveled hovels without architectural passages or in hotels with intellectual passengers without articulate messages or on over-booked steamship passages without International travelers where "mosh-pit" messages discreetly announce "free bees, frisbees and bonuses" such as "hot-dog" sausages and "cool cat" massages. *Gemutlich.*

181

A Noble Man for a Nobel Prize.

Now without being told in the MANner of speech or in the
WOMANer of writings, the hypocritical, non-unique critics with
their highly critical *critiques,* will ignobly announce that the
next Nobel Prize-Winner will be a noble-wise astonisher not
an ignoble-sized admonisher, an adult not an adulterer, a one-
night Adventist not an one week adventurer, an almoner not a
confectioner, a native road-sweeper not a foreign gate-keeper,
a questioner not an answerer, an arbitrator not an arbiter, an
arbitrageur not a traitor, an armorer not a charmer, an astrologer
not an astronomer, an autographer not an autobiographer, a
biographer not a bibliographer, a lender not a borrower, a sewer
not a broiderer, an enlightener not a burdener, a banterer not a
chatterer, a barterer not a bickerer, a challenger not a cricketer,
a banqueter not a confectioner, a barrister not a counselor, a
biographer not a councilor, a banterer not a carpenter, a caterer
not a bargainer, a cherisher not a chorister, a commoner not a
chronicler, a comforter not a coroner, a fumbler not a conjurer,
a dowager not a cottager, an emblazoner not an embellisher,
an encourager not a discourager, an endeavourer not an
engenderer, an enchanter not a disenchanter, an examiner
not an executioner, a fashioner not a favorer, a flatterer not a
flutterer, a forager not a forester, a gardener not a gatherer, a
harborer not a harbinger, a photographer not a lithographer, a

gossiper not a jabberer, a loiterer not a galloper, an uplander
not a lowlander, a Neanderthal not a Netherlander, a Lady Lucy
not a shady Lucifer, a manager not a manufacturer, a mariner
not a malingerer, a milliner not a manager, a stark murmurer
with a heart murmur but not a marked murderer, a modeler not
a yodeler, a measurer not a messenger, a userer not an utterer,
a mutterer not a stutterer, a parishioner not a passenger, a
pasturer not a plasterer, a pepperer not a salter, a pensioner not
a petitioner, a pesterer not a perjurer, a Presbyterian practitioner
rather than Dan Rather the Anglican probationer, lodger Phil
the philogerer Rather Dan dodger Artful the philosopher, the
Elvis phonographer Rather Dan the pelvis photographer, a
poster posturer Rather Dan a paltry poulterer, a handsome
ransomer Dan Rather rather than a seasoned Harry Reasoner,
a reversioner not a relinquisher, an all-day reveler to an all-night
rioter but what's an all-steel hull to Billy Hill the hillbilly riveter,
what's a sauntering roisterer doing in the Cloister watching a
scavanger with a scimitar, skirmishing in the Sepulcher with a
Westminster Minister most sinister, better chance winning than
sinning, being a slumberer than a slaughterer, a savage ravager
rather than a ravished savager, a publisher not a punisher, a
purse-chaser not a purchaser, a quarreler not a quaverer, a
pilferer not a pillager, a plasterer not a plunderer, a polisher
not a porridger, a wittier not a pittier, a railway stationer not

a stationary probationer, a topographer not a typographer, an investor not a idolater, an interpreter not an imprisoner, a harvester not a languisher, a lecturer not a lavisher, a lecturer not a libeler, a lithographer not a stenographer, a slanderer than a libeler, a sister sophister not a cup on a saucer, a milliner not a sorcerer, a stammering stutterer with a pitiful putter, a suffering succorer not a puffing swaggerer, a Savannah dampener not a Tampa Bay tamperer, preferred a Bikini Atoll "don't-lie-on-me" babe in a spotless bikini, to a Miami Beach "don't-die-on-me" socialite with her ex-husband's "beanie," loved tall topless broads layered in sun-tan oil creamy, and settled down with short bottomless broads who were broad where a broad should be broad and their young blue eyes dreamy. No slouch on the couch with a "casting couch" actress, her manner didactic with nylons elastic, her bosom most plastic, her dandy in aspic, a very tricky "Tricky Dick" director with a TV and a prompter, who had to romp her 'till he prompt her to study the studio Tele-Prompter, but most likely a traveler not a torturer, a treasurer not a trespasser, a trumpeter not a tetrameter, an upholsterer not a typographer, a usurer not an utterer, a villager not a victualer, a valuer not a vanquisher, a voyager not a visitor, a wanderer not a wagoner, a wassalier not a wagerer, a whisperer not a whimperer, an outsider not an inner, a tenor not a tinner, a fatter not thinner, a saint not a sinner, a true evangelist not a

Benny Hinn-er, a Yang-er not a Ying-er, a "here now" not a has-binner, a binary not a linear, a buttoner not a pin-er, a canner not a bin-er, a laugher not a grinner, a whisky drinker not a gin-er, with His excoriate thinner, played His plays Inn Trinity Hall and was announced as the winner by the Dallas Poets Society just after dinner. *Festschrift.*

Have a Good Look at Me Now.................

And with that the *Scholastic Irishman* was gone, disappeared in the same way that he arrived, like a ship on the ocean, an evening star, a non-boring *borealis,* from the brightest yellow-poppy, bell-red geranium of a day to the darkest seldom-choppy, well read cranium of the night, that was it, *kaputfallen, gefertig, hellas, no mas, pau.* Gone was His usual agonistical adventitiousness, very characteristical judiciousness, precise egostical capriciousness, delightful egotistical meritriciousness, biting Calvanistical perniciousness, insightful alchemistical fictitioness, rabid theosophistical superstitiousness, benign-design cathechistical inauspiciousness, flamboyant artistical auspiciousness, secret cabalistical seditiousness, unrequieted euphemistical propitiousness, tongue-twisting linguistical deliciousness, enthusiastic atheistical capriciousness, non-ending dialogistical avariciousness, openly theistical suppositiousness, wholly eucharistical suspiciousness, very methodistical expeditiousness, a literary giant disappeared without a trace, and without a trace of antagonistical maliciousness and anarchistical viciousness..........

For After I'm Gone.....................

Somewhat an anomalistical traditionist, a statistical requisitionist, a antarchistical prohibitionist, a sophistical coalitionist, a puristical abolitionist, an aoristical exhibitionist, a mystical oppositionist, and an apathistical expeditionist. He was ever the aphoristical traditional, the pietistical volitional, the casuistical intuitional, the paragraphistical inquisitional, the chemistical definitional, the hemistical propositional, the eulogistical prepositional, not to mention a deistical repetitional of pieces of Heavenly Peace. Never got the rhyme right at the Rhymers' Club, always got the limelight at the Irish National Theatre Society, never got up before the Hermetic Order of the Golden Dawn, was ever an initiate, maleficiate, novitiate, patriciate, propitiate, vitiate, of the Esoteric section of the Theosophical Society, but was never-once asked if he would like to officiate...............

You'll Ne'er Ever See the Likes O'Me Again.

The Irish admonitioner, the literary coalitioner, the modern-verse commissioner, the sonnet-spewing exhibitioner, the potato-peeling missioner, the Worldly practitioner, the wordly traditioner; the excitative, incitative, writative genius at literary prose, rhyming verse, poetic literature; his flightiness and mightiness from the Great Almighty, where did he come from (nobody knows), where has he gone to (only God knows), his no-body nose sniffing pheromes of Heavenly hue, a consistory history but no answer to the mystery, never again such an explicitness, illicitness, implicitness, and licentious licit-ness with all it's solitude, solicitude and vicissitude, where else can be found such omnipresence, omnificence, omnifariousness, omnium-gatherum, omnipotence and omniscience ?

Depart Im Augenblick.

In a flash, in a twinkle of an eye, not even Yeats's horseman had time to glance a backward eye. I hope you all had a good time now, for we'll never read the likes of Him again. So Arrivederci, Ashoge, Shukran, Shnorhagallem, Doh je, Wa'-do, Mese, Danku, Tashakkur, Paljon kiitoksia, Merci beaucoup, Danke schon, Sas efharisto, Toda, Shukriya, Terima kasih, Ta, Arigato, Kasaare, Asante, Dhanyawaada, Gratia tibi ago, Achiu, Xie xie, Tand ikh bayarlalaa, Tusen takk, Dsiejuje, Dhannvaad, Spasibo, Tapadh leibh, Hvala, Muchas gratias, Jag tackar, Khawp khun, Tesekkurler, and Dyakooyu.

Go Raibh Maith Agat and Slan Abhaile.

About the Author

Leon O'Chruadhlaoich was born at a very early age of Celtic parents in the English West Country, writing his first poems in the shadow of Gloucestershire's Gustav Holst, Oxfordshire's William Shakespeare, Worcestershire's Sir Edward Elgar and England's Poet Laureate John Masefield, the Herefordshire wordsmith. As an exceptionally gifted athlete and scholarly youth, he academically excelled in the Scholastic Sciences and for over a decade delightfully and insightfully indulged some of his well-spent couth in the ramifications and study of PsychoNeuroEndocrineImmunology in the Earl of Sandwich Islands. Although having the disadvantage of a formal education and an Ivy League graduation, he persevered as a writer *honorarium,* writing more and more about less and less until he ended up writing everything about nothing. When approached ante-humorously and extremely posthumously by Mr. James Joyce, very late of Rathgar, County Dublin, Ireland in late 2002, the author found *The Scholastic Irishman* all pervasive when invisible but all persuasive when visible, and condescended to complete the previous attempts at "ghost-writing" by American authors Sloan Wilson and Anthony Burgess. Despite Mr. Joyce's rejoicing, the author insisted (because of his day job) that the work would be presented in a stream of un-interrupted sub-consciousness rather than in *The Scholastic Irishman's* growth-industry, time-consuming, self-exiled, physician-phobic, wife-devoted, stream of interrupted consciousness. The deal was done and the cow ate the cabbage. If the author knew that he was going to be so exalted amongst the peoples, he would have taken better care of himself. He currently is a resident of Dallas, Texas, USA and since 2004 has performed Joyce's the two plays encapsulated here every June 16 onstage, the last *thrice anni* at the Trinity Hall Pub and Restaurant, astride Central Expressway and Mockingbird Lane. He recites in the night at home beneath the Preston Hollow steeple-spire, observes the flame of a Delphic candle in the sheltered, blue cardinal winged-bower, writes pomes *dolareach* in the poppy-sun, rabbit-run, squirrel-patch, mockingbird-calling, leafy cottonwood shade, and lives alone, very peacefully, under the leaf-covered shower, the humming-bird whirring, the early-bird stirring, the seldom-seen scene, less-traveled boreen, in Billy Yeats' bee-loud glade.